THE DRUNK, THE GAMBLER, AND THE LOVER

EMBER WHITE

Copyright © 2025.

All rights reserved. This book or parts thereof may not be reproduced in any form, stored in any retrieval system, or transmitted in any form by any means—electronic, mechanical, photocopy, recording, or otherwise—without prior written permission of the publisher, except as provided by United States of America copyright law.

Cover Illustration: Marta Maszkiewicz

ISBN: 978-1-950321-56-8

TABLE OF CONTENTS

Chapter 1: Greed Is Good 5

Chapter 2: Faceless 9

Chapter 3: The Feast 14

Chapter 4: A Calculus of Emotions 19

Chapter 5: Faith and Logic 25

Chapter 6: Self-Acceptance 34

Chapter 7: Play to Play 42

Chapter 8: The Painting and the Machine 51

Chapter 9: The Empty Glass 60

Chapter 10: A Stranger in a Void 70

Chapter 11: Demon 78

Chapter 12: The Lover 87

About the Author 95

CHAPTER ONE:

GREED IS GOOD

The Drunk slowly but surely remembered and subsequently why it took so long to remember. It was late afternoon. There was no reason to arise, and nothing stirred an instinct to move.

There was no headache, no nausea, no vertigo, but also no desire. It was a state of perfect contentment and discontentment, a sort of befuddled enlightenment. Nothing truly mattered but being, which was more than enough.

What The Drunk was, looked like, and wore were of no importance, especially to The Drunk. In fact, few things mattered at all.

Hours later, as if running on a tight train schedule, thirst and hunger returned. The Drunk sat up, softly planted feet on the floor, and stood up, finding no satisfaction in the miracle that had just taken place. A not-so-quick descent down the stairs led to the common area of the house which was shared alongside several tenants, all of which were entirely nameless but one. The Gambler was there preparing his afternoon coffee.

"You're late," The Gambler spoke.

"Late for what?" The Drunk asked with a growing cheerfulness.

"Just later than usual is all."

"You know, getting up at five everyday isn't so bad. I don't see why people complain about it so much."

"Five o'clock in the afternoon. Truly, truly brilliant. So, then, how will you follow this extraordinary feat?"

"Work as always. I work everyday, don't you remember? I mean, what else would I do? Oh, and could you make me a cup as well?"

"Of course," answered The Gambler. "And I'll say it again, then. I think it's fantastic that you work hard everyday in spite of all else. It's something I aspire to do myself as well."

By then, the newly ground coffee, pure distilled water, and sturdy machine were all in their proper places ready to brew. A switch was flipped on.

"Work is not everything, but I think we are both aware of that by this point. For myself, I write till I can write no longer, and then I drink." The Drunk explained as had been explained to all while this time parked on top of the forgettable sofa, looking out the usual window and then, sensing comfort in The Gambler's presence, relocated to the dining table, ready for coffee and conversation.

"What are you writing right now?"

"I'm still working on that same biography, sadly. There's so much research involved, which means progress has been annoyingly slow. But it will be all worth it in the end, you know. These kinds of stories sell incredibly well. The other day, I showed you that one leading in sales right now, do you remember? Great title, genius marketing, mediocre book. If I could only finish this book and deliver something better. I know the marketing; I've gone

Chapter One: Greed Is Good

and made so many books by now that the entire process is habit, more or less. And you've seen my past work. It will sell, I tell you."

"And yet after all those books, you are still stuck here with me. Well done. But let's say this book does sell. Do you think you'll finally have enough to quit your laboring job then?"

"That depends. How much is enough? When is enough enough? Is it one million or two?"

A subtle smile washed over The Gambler's face. "Allow me to answer your question with another question. Do you want to make money, or do you want to make more money? Why stop there? Why not accumulate as much as you can while you *still* can? Don't you see it's in our bones?"

"Have you never overworked yourself before? Are we soaked sponges to be willingly wrung out again and again?"

"I have no objection to that, and some days I would like nothing more. At least, then, I would be too exhausted to do anything senseless. Temptation never truly leaves you, you know? It's always there, and it's always waiting for me. A mere hour trip and I'm at the casino, a lair for all things no good. Come three o'clock in the morning, and there I am, seething after being parted with whatever lump of cash I decided to bring. The tide can be brutal, and even when you've carefully calculated the odds to be in your favor with every wager you make, you can still lose it all." The Gambler puckered in his lips slightly.

The coffee had been fully prepared and dispensed. Its smell sprayed the room with the scent of roasted vanilla and an impending pleasure. A cup was filled, and a switch was flipped off.

"And it's always the hard-fought wins that bring me back. There's nothing quite like it. You can only go on so many walks and read so many books, I suppose. Anyways, I'm off to my office to follow up with a few leads I have. Good luck to you and your writing."

Ember White

    The Drunk's eyes trailed along and up the stairs and towards the ceiling until a door was slammed. It was past ready for morning coffee. And so feet shuffled, hands grabbed the thoroughly stained cup, and legs side-stepped to the sturdy machine. It was empty.
    Eyes stared at the drying pot without the slightest flinch. The brows were motionless. A mind preoccupied with thoughts of what lay ahead that day had little room for much else. The writing to be done was going to sour the tongue again as it had for some time. All the hours would be spent and only to cough up half of a deadbeat passage by the end.
    This would be due to no distraction. All entertainment had run its course by this point. If there was any diversion remaining, it would be of the mind itself, and the watcher of the mind was too tired to control it any further. Desire now softly rang outwards without direction and to no one particular thing, merely embracing the corner of every room all while faintly disturbed. Money was vaguely needed, yet it came with the envy of days of past fulfillment. What was gone was gone, and it was to never come back. What was here was here to stay, and it was unfulfilled.
    A large draft outside broke The Drunk's brooding thoughts. Eyes peered out the window to see a breath of wind rustle fragile branches and their whirling tendrils. There was a symphony of wavering and dances and even a slight bobbling and nodding from the higher and lower branches that seemed to be also watching with full interest. Life moved and flourished along while the eyes moved downward to the reluctant trunk. A pang of jealous desire rippled down the spine.
    Pen and pad were retrieved and placed upon The Drunk's private writing desk. Many hours passed. And after a full day of work, the mind had indeed produced a paltry unfinished passage and called it a day. A cabinet door was forcibly opened, and glasses came forth.

CHAPTER TWO:

FACELESS

The factory belt never stopped. It had no brain to reason with or heart to compel. But it had ears that could listen. The Drunk often spoke to it, revealing dark troubles and woes over a period of hours and hours, eager for answers. A few came while most did not, but a gradual numbing and release from the disease of thinking was assured.

The belt never stopped, but it would never leave either. And it would not judge; it would not condemn. It could not be caught snickering or sneering. The Drunk would tell it the most offensive jokes and take the mechanical gurgling for its giddy, girlish laughter. Dear friends had come and gone but never the belt. It was the greatest listener of all, a companion like no other.

These thoughts and more kept The Drunk occupied for the next nine hours. It was not aches or pains but weakness of body and spirit that defined this morning. And it was pointless to pay any attention to a mind vowing never to do this or never to do that. Rather, to focus on the franken-droning of the belt was far more productive. At least, then, one could practice being a good listener themselves and aspire to create a deeper relationship with the belt.

There were other laborers around of course, but it was not as if these persons were faceless. It was, in fact, The Drunk who was faceless. To go out into the world was to show one's face, and The Drunk had no face to show. There were eyes, a nose, cheeks, and a mouth, but the whole was disfigured and misshapen. Yet no one would see and say there was any abnormality. One might even say it was healthy, youthful, lean, attractive, or perhaps even beautiful. To The Drunk, however, it was not just useless; it brought pain. It brought the wrong kind of attention. Any interaction was the wrong interaction. Connections were superficial and lies at best or hurtful and even cruel at their worst, all stemming from false assumptions about a nameless, faceless, formless, or in other words, isolated soul. Even relations with The Gambler were only possible with a willingness to understand that the face was indeed disfigured and a result of misfortune.

There was one other who demonstrated a similar willingness. After the hours passed with fatigue and the shift had ended, The Drunk sat at a table outside the factory awaiting a certain companion. It was then The Lover appeared and took his usual seat across.

"You asked me for my true opinion about your book, so here, I'll give it to you. You write this biography, but it's just empty knowledge. Exposition won't change how a person feels. Besides, there's enough, no, there's too much information out there. It's all mind, and all the mind will do is make you miserable." He thus spoke and then firmly leaned back to let his words air themselves out.

As The Drunk was listening, a stupid grin grew and stretched like rubber across the loose face, and in silence, the lips continued to extend outward as far as to seemingly try to make their escape.

"What? What are you smiling about?" The Lover couldn't help but begin to replicate the infectious grin.

Chapter Two: Faceless

"I could give you a rock, and you would tell me everything that is wrong with it."

"No. I have no problems with no rock. It's humanity that is dead from the neck up. 'Oh, look at me! I have all this wealth and power, come see! Look at the wasteful clutter I now have! Oh, look at me, all of you! Look at how I support this noble and lofty cause, and see how good I am.'"

The Drunk had been reduced to a pile of giggling, broken by brashness and absurdity. After an inhale of crisp, cool air, there was a pause to reset the mood.

"Well, what am I supposed to write? This biography is all I know. There's no grand epic floating around in my head. Even if there was, I'd write it, finish it, and be right back to where I started."

"Exactly. That is why you must live instead."

"And I live to work. Work is the only way I know how to live. Nothing else seems to be able to quite do it. And it can be very fulfilling, you know."

The Lover parted his lips to interject but quickly withdrew and closed them. He looked away into the vague distance while a new line of thinking took hold, and his head pivoted back.

"There was this new face today. Did you see her?"

"I think so. Wait, are we thinking of the same one?"

"I don't know. You go first."

"The plainly dressed girl with the glasses."

"Oh, so you think that one's the most beautiful, then? Well, well, well." The Lover hung on to his last word as it evaporated across his cheeks, leaving behind a fat, impish smirk.

"You know," The Drunk uttered, stopping before steering the conversation into a sore corner. Thoughts realigned themselves and continued. "I was sure we both picked the same one. But tell me, who were you thinking of?"

"There was a group of three of them. You saw them, right?"

"Yes."

"It's not the one with the painted face. Those are the ones who have the most to hide. It's also not the younger one with the glasses: too conventional. But oh, is it that last one."

"You mean her?"

"She," The Lover said with his elbow gently grazing the table away from his body. His arm then parked into place while his heavy head rested in his palm with a single finger to stroke his cheek. "Someone like that is someone who does not stop everything but accelerates it. My heart found a new rhythm, one it's never known, and all feeling is double the feeling now. When I even look at her, there's this firm pressure to perform and succeed."

"I remember now. You like the sultry ones."

"Fecundity!" shouted The Lover, lightly striking the table with the palm that was nestling his heavy head.

"Fecundity?"

"Yes!"

Unsure of how to respond, The Drunk froze in hesitation as a slow, frivolous smile unfurled across the face. The smile then cracked into a half-suppressed laughter. The air lightened, and permission was given for adults to play as children again. A fit of mirth was released, much like a child releases a balloon, only to watch it slowly shrink into a cerulean sky.

"I do have to be running off, but I wish you good luck in your chase."

"Same time next week, then."

After parting ways and completing a few simple errands about town and finally arriving home, The Drunk was too exhausted for anything else meaningful. Even a drink would go wholly unnoticed

Chapter Two: Faceless

at this late of an hour. And so the body lay in bed, fully prepared for sleep.

One minute had passed. The head had become awfully uneasy. The lone spirit lying in the discomfort of the bed had only a willowy blanket to hide behind. It was not enough. An accumulated pain came forth from the unconscious and the unknown and took root across the entire body and at last the chamber of the heart.

The lips trembled. They motioned to speak but only a soft whimper could be made out. The mind willingly stepped in to speak for the sober soul.

"I cannot love," it said. "There is nothing to love or even hate. This body cannot love. This body has never loved. How could it love when I feel nothing for no one? No one is more than a bag of flesh to be hung and sold at the butcher's market. No one is anything. No one. No one."

The Drunk bubbled and bubbled and then bled emotions through dispirited tears, thus collapsing and passing peacefully into a deep and restful sleep.

CHAPTER THREE:

THE FEAST

      Another day of writing awaited The Drunk. There was passion but no words. A complete story had been captured but without the will to translate it to paper. The writer who did not write was then a waster of time and talent, a retired fire kindler, an admirer of windows, and an icon for all work-shy youth.

    The Drunk abandoned forceful thinking long ago. The ideas needed now could no longer be searched for. They merely occurred. The work was then to be patient and catch them. There was sitting and waiting and waiting and sitting. Acting and doing were prohibited, for occupied eyes could not see what busy hands could not catch.

    Nothing occurred. Time passed, and more things did not occur. All life seemed to be occurring elsewhere. Gatherings were taking place between friends new and old, forming crystalline memories that could stand up to even the fear of old age, sickness, and death, preparing a well-lived life to pass easily into the next. Lovers were breaching past their hearts and exposing their most vulnerable souls to one another, thereby coupling themselves

Chapter Three: The Feast

together until they were as unbreakable as diamonds. Even colleagues were somehow fulfilling each other's bare needs for human connection while bonding through mutual suffering or even hatred.

The Drunk waned in focus, and the mind was now dull. There was no reason to push against something that now resisted. Work was sacred, but there was nothing sacred left this day.

No drink or even food had been taken all day. And there was no purpose in abstaining beyond this point.

As The Drunk was preparing a range of bottles and glasses in the common area of the house, The Gambler, too, was preparing his own banquet. And so an impromptu feast was naturally in order.

They gathered in The Gambler's private quarters. Two glasses of an excellent smokey Islay scotch were poured for such an occasion and given time to open up, just as a glass of wine.

"If you have to explain why a book is so great before I read it so that I might get it, that really doesn't sell me on the idea," said The Gambler with a starved fork in hand.

"You could be right, yes. Rather, I think I'm in love with the story of the writer than his actual book. It's this story of a person who fears they have wasted the whole of their life away, but somehow, someway, they find a way to remember it all and see that was not the case."

The Gambler slowed his chewing to deliver a brief nod and thought. "A life should not waste your time. A life should make you want to waste your time."

"I can drink to that," spoke The Drunk with fingers twirling around a glass.

The two toasted and downed a sip of the scotch poured earlier, which was now in full bloom. The Gambler raised his eyebrows in mere satisfaction. The Drunk leaned back as the head lightly spun involuntarily, mesmerized by flavors of joy and blessedness; the head rattled left and right and left and right again as the tongue related the secrets to happiness and folly that have been long lost and forgotten.

"You always catch me by surprise with that face. Tell me, how can you drink so much but eat so little? I sit here with my fried this and baked that, and you, you nibble away at your raw lettuces like a rabbit."

"That's very simple. I do like to drink and have no reason not to do so. But I also like my small-boned physique so I eat as little as possible."

"Still, I admire that discipline. To me, if I can just satiate every desire as soon as I have it, why not? Especially when I have the money, I don't see why not."

"Really? You've never eaten a great deal and then immediately watch it become a great deal of regret?"

"That, too, passes, and I somehow manage to keep forgetting." The Gambler let out a light but hearty snort.

"That I do understand. It's built into our nature, and so we keep coming back," The Drunk replied while the eyes glossed over the large collection of bottles. "But you do aspire to many things. You've told me before of the life you wish to build with that fortune you'll have one day. I believe in it."

"I will have the money one day, yes. And I will buy that property. And then I will buy another and then this residence and that residence. That's the dream, and oh, it will be out of this world. Of course the wealth is perfectly nice, but then, I'll be playing the game of estates; and won't that be a life of its own? I'll be snatching up territory after territory, like a lord, and collecting the profits from my army of serfs. I'll take care of them, and they'll take care of me. And I do mean that. There are good causes I'd like to support as well."

Chapter Three: The Feast

"That's quite a lot, and you've had only but one drink as well. But you'll eventually get there by playing at the big tables, is that right?"

"Yes, and honestly, that's why I strive for that discipline, at least at the table." The Gambler gently laid his starved fork to rest. "Poker is all about patience and calculation and stamina. It's a game where you must slowly figure out your opponents and how they play before they do you. Are they betting only when they have something and for how much? When are they bluffing and for how much? Or are they so good that they know exactly when and how to bluff so that you can never quite predict what they might have? Get emotional, and they'll read you front to back cover. Bet everything too soon, and you'll lose it all. I may be impulsive in life, but I fight it when sitting at that table. It means too much to me."

The Drunk rubbed hands for comfort as ears listened to each word while attention struggled with that familiar air of restlessness, which followed from room to room during long nights. An effort, an anxious effort, was made to hold out as The Gambler explained the complete intricacies and nuances of the game. If waiting was hard now, future times would only then be truly more difficult. So The Drunk sat and waited and rocked and waited. Moments and even seconds had gone by and then a minute.

The compromised spirit had listened for quite long enough, and hands reached for a new glass. Great spirits were too valuable to allow to sully in a used glass where flavors would be contaminated.

"Addictive, I'm sure."

Soon after many rounds of drinking, the feast adjourned and was to reconvene on some vague future night. The Drunk lay in bed, having thoroughly quenched all anxieties with whiskey and food. It was a dulling embrace, an intimate numbness, and a paradoxical solution.

Ember White

Two lowly notes etched out in a pad from earlier that day sat upon the nearby desk. And all else was without worth. Past deeds and efforts were closeted while walls displayed barrenness. Thoughts of value were muddled into disorder as drunken sleep quickly overtook all.

CHAPTER FOUR:

A CALCULUS OF EMOTIONS

Today, no passages were to be written. It was time for work. It had been several days since The Drunk had left the house. Well-rested steps sprang forth with buttery glee and without a trace of gloom.

A self-imposed prisoner was afforded the simple pleasure of being made to leave the confines to roam the courtyard once again. There, labor would be required on the part of the prisoner, but for crisp air, room and reason to move and stretch, and a rolled cigarette, the price was small. There would even be other prisoners to converse with or merely just gaze at with a mildly curious eye, all without the threat of violence. If The Drunk was ever released, which had been the case many times before, the temptation to reoffend and return was all too much, for today's thought was that life may be ample and great even in a prison.

Menial tasks numbed the mind but were craved by the body. The evolution of work was set in reverse, for no longer was labor centered around a motionless desk. There was now bending, binding, bundling, carting, cleaning, climbing, cutting, delivering, dropping, folding, forcing, grasping, gripping, kneeling, lifting, packing, picking, peeling, pivoting, pressing, pulling, pushing, reaching, ripping, sealing, squatting, squeezing, sticking, taping, tossing, turning, twisting, and, most of all, walking.

And there was a simple joy to be found in it all. A well-worked body could always rest satisfied, while an ambitious mind may hardly ever with its visions of complete works that haunted its creator until they were utterly finished and even sickening to look any further and thus finally ready to be let go of.

Work was sacred, even if found in a factory, for where there was work, there was a reason not to drink. The pay was poor, yet the soul was rich. A willful writer had long perished, and a lowly laborer had been reborn in place. There were yet worse things in life than indentured servitude. And if they were ever so bad once more, a vision of grandeur would come again as it had before. And there were nine hours each day to mull and stew and cook.

The clock struck the end of shift, bringing work to a close. The Drunk made way to the usual meeting place outside the factory and awaited the company of a certain fellow laborer. It was not long before the two met once more.

"She quit," said The Lover.

"Are you sure?"

"I'm sure of it. I haven't seen her all week."

"That's a loss for us both, then."

"Sad. I won't—I'm not quite myself today."

"Yes, I can see it. What will you do then?"

"There's a cafe not too far from here. I know the owners there, and they know me. Good people. They make the most delicious waffles I've ever had at the most unpretentious cafe I've ever been. You know how much I despise fancy and showy. But there, I'll have my meal and gather myself again." The Lover's words were firm yet spoken at a pace much slower than normal. He rested his head on his weary arms themselves already resting on the table.

Chapter Four: A Calculus of Emotions

"I'll then go home, and do what I always do, turn to books, of course. An old book is like having a conversation with an old friend. They've been dead for hundreds of years, but it's the truest talk you've ever had."

"It's been a long day," replied The Drunk. The other nodded while not breaking eye contact with the table. "Tell me. What do you like to read?"

"The types that make you feel something again. It doesn't need to be pretty or beautiful. In fact, the more degenerate the better. Show me the dark, and show me its truth. Just give me characters, not worlds. Other than that, nothing else matters. Write about whatever you like, just not non-fiction. It all reads like fiction these days and not the good kind."

"You must like poetry, then."

The Lover slowly lifted his head with renewed energy. "Of course. That's the direct window into the heart. How often do we speak with feeling anymore? No one does anymore. It's all repeated and recited intellectual rubbish. And now, everyone speaks like a man. But if I read someone's poems, let's say, I know everything there is to know about that person. There is no deeper you can go, and any information you tell me about them before or after is pointless."

The Drunk paused in reflection. "I wish I could write such a thing. I've made many attempts before, but I never have enough. There is a story I have to tell, but I can't ever seem to find the right metaphor for it."

"Metaphors, yes. That's how you do it! Even Jesus taught using parables."

"But I don't have a parable either. Do you? Do you write?"

"You could say that, but that was some time ago. There was a time I wanted to create something truly great and massive. I was like you in your search, reading every classic I could get my hands on and always mulling and stewing. Then one day, I realized this—this life bolted and barred away in my room wasn't what I wanted. It wasn't going to make me happy any longer. All this toil and labor and years of sacrifice was now leaving me tired and miserable. And worst of all, I felt utterly alone. No. No, that wasn't what I wanted at all," The Lover spoke these last words while stubbornly but softly shaking his head as if to give the surest answer he ever had.

The Drunk's brow invisibly pulsed upon hearing the words *tired*, *miserable*, and *alone*. "I see. Maybe one day then. One day, after you have lived a full life, perhaps then, it will drop right into your heavy head, and you'll catch it. I do like to think that everyone has at least one good book in them. It's just a matter of translating it onto paper."

"I must live first. You know, before any of this, I was a degenerate."

"Oh, is that so?" The Drunk lightly smiled.

"I've thrown my life away by doing nothing but studying this game and that game, and I'm tired of the mind and its silly games. I have not truly lived, and that is what I want, above all. I want more out of life!" As The Lover was finishing his thoughts, he delivered a firm chop to the table with the palm of his hand.

"You should. Yes, you are right in what you want. The more we die before we die the more we have lived."

A short pause became a few moments of silence. The sun had stretched out its maiden arms below and warmly caressed the table and its two visitors. The sky was perfectly clear and its beauty taken for granted as always until this very moment. And a feint motorized humming was somehow just as natural as well.

"I will have her," The Lover said, breaking the stillness.

"Who?"

"Her. I just have to find her first. And I then will claim her using something very few men have. She and all women know and speak a language that no man can truly understand. It's a calculus of emotions innate to them that does not need to be taught. Men nowadays approach a girl with cold reason and hard logic and then wonder why she has no interest in him. But a man can fully conquer his own emotions, however, and learn to speak through them, in fact. He can serenade her with nothing but his own feelings and soul fire. That is what I must do. There is no other way for me."

"You are an intense one, aren't you? You're never one to waste your words."

The Lover blinked. "Do you think it's too much?"

"Oh, not at all. I like those that speak from their soul. How often do you meet someone who says everything you have heard somewhere else before and nothing truly original? Every word and opinion they have is parroted and hidden behind some personality. You can almost predict everything they say before it even leaves their mouth."

"Yes," said The Lover with eyes once more shimmering with life. "And the worst of it, the part that sears me more than the rest, is fake politeness, that—that fake kindness people feel they have to extend you because of some make-believe obligation. And the reality is they don't care for you. They don't care one lick about you even. They think they're doing the virtuous thing and are being a good person, and yet they also think no one sees through their act. It's disgusting, really."

Impassioned words were met with the silence of mellowed agreement. This silence, however, was longer than the last; it signaled the wane of conversation. Everything needed to be said had been said, and every desire to be heard had been heard. The two stood up and exchanged their farewells.

Later that night, The Drunk had completed the day's tasks and was preparing supper for the evening. There was thirst but no hunger. Seven nights of drinking were counted this week, and hunger had been absent for the past few. Past temptations arose.

There were no greater drams than those several years ago. Days of endless writing to unsee what had been seen were followed by long nights of wondrous, magnificent drams to forget it all. Everything wrong with this world was everything right with that glass. Work was sacred. Money was hope. Whiskey was holy. Food was an accessory.

Never will a dram taste that good once more as it had on those nights. The Drunk vowed it. Food was always to be served before any drink, and tonight was no exception; the swollen liver pleaded as much.

The Drunk, now full of wheat bread and wheated bourbon, passed into an easy sleep. There then was a dream, which came in the form of a broken, incoherent stream of consciousness.

"Write. Don't look at it. Write. It's staring from across the room. Write. It won't stop staring. It doesn't blink. Write. It moved. Where did it go? It's now behind you. Write. Why did you look? Write. Yes, write. Write more. Why are you afraid? It's just you. It's just you looking at you. Write. Don't think. Write. Yes, but its head is titled. Write. It's tilted like that forever. And it's you. Don't you remember? You promised me. Write. Write faster than the day before. It's you from all those years ago. Look, you did it. Write. Write this book faster than any before it. And it will be done, just like you. No. Stop crying. Write. Write. It won't go away. It follows from room to room. Write. Write harder. Why is it on the floor? Why is there blood? You don't go away. That's right. Don't go away. Now write."

CHAPTER FIVE:

FAITH AND LOGIC

With a few extra hours of sleep, the worst of the morning had become the best of the morning. Without second thought, The Drunk ploddingly crept out of bed and was then seated at the work desk in the corner of the room.

There was a glowing hum that started from deep within and covered the body in a radiant warmth. Its source was not the heart but somewhere just below it. The still mind stood tranquilized by the morning glow, knowing its thoughts were nothing more than splashes in an ocean of bliss. Hours walked by the sitting body, and no desires surfaced save for the company of a morning cup.

Together they would stare a thousand yards into the distance, seeking truth, piercing every wall of concrete and Earth in their line of vision and wandering into the infinity. These truths were not known but felt and so powerful that no soul could move in their presence. And so the body sat. Yet it did not wait, for there was no need of waiting. This moment and the next were immaculate.

Ember White

Alas, morning could not stay and was now going, taking along its soft blissful buzzing with it. The rest of the day began to settle in. The mind began to bore the heart with its endless thoughts and worries. Soon, some kind of work was to be in order. It was a Saturday evening, and The Drunk knew only of one kind of work to be done: it would be writing; for it was all that was known. All else had been long forgotten. Worldly life had connected the writer to nothing but an inner world.

The unfinished book begged and nagged, but The Drunk was too poor to hand out more than a line or two. If the heart turned away, cheap words could be ground up, packaged into a product, and marketed as a centerpiece of culture. With enough money put in and the right persons paid off, it would sell millions of copies, and the masses would be taught to praise its simplicity. Immense prosperity and ampleness would be achieved; material life would cease to be a problem evermore, and its creator would gradually descend into misery and shame once more for having deceived oneself and the world.

The Drunk would not and could not produce such a thing. To make the latest work better than the last was ideal.

Ideals did nothing, however, to move the pen across the page. It scribbled and scratched and staggered with the task at hand. It didn't move through fire, like it once had, yet it still moved. There was a sentence then another then another. The integrity was there, although slow.

By the middle, it couldn't be helped but to think if there was some unseen path that branched off the current. It mattered not where this path led, and it could even be longer than the current one. It merely needed to be one where movement was free and absolute once again. The goal was neither the end nor the adventure but movement and life itself.

Chapter Five: Faith and Logic

After a full day of writing, The Drunk was keeping busy by meticulously setting and arranging bottles in a U-shape on the common room table. One row was dedicated to all the various types of scotches, organized by the region in which they were produced in Scotland. Another row was for the not-so-popular but oh-so-rich and unique line of rye whiskies. And the final row contained the famed and renowned wall of bourbons and their intimate flavors such recognized by so many.

Through a pristine drinking glass, The Gambler could be seen making his way to the common room.

"That's quite the selection of bottles there, but really now, don't tell me that's all you have."

The Drunk smiled. "Of course not. You know me better than that. I couldn't decide what to have today, so I've built myself a small cathedral with all the stained glasses here. Inside, there are no sermons or priests, only temporary sanctuary from the aches and pains of a troubled soul. All are welcome here in my church where I will pour you a glass, any glass, and you may unburden yourself with whatever may be weighing heavily on you."

"I'll pass, thank you. I'll have a coffee instead."

"If I remember, you are not religious, is that right?"

"God, no. So many people then ask me, 'Why not? Why not?' and I simply tell them this: I don't believe. That tends to shut down most pretty quickly."

"That seems very clear and firm to me, like you've made up your mind long ago, but then, there's always those that can't take no for an answer."

"Those—with those, now, I just can't help myself," spoke The Gambler while narrowly cocking his chin up to one side. "Just the other day, I was resting during my hike up one of the mountains to the west here when I had a talk with these two Evangelicals passing by. I was immediately invited to join their church and their meetings and the such and the like; and it was they who riled me up and left me with no choice. And I let them have it. It had all turned into a bitter debate almost naturally. Now, in the back of my mind, I know they can't be talked out of a position they did not rationally talk themselves into, but then, they began using logic to justify their faith. God, it was utterly annoying. It was the as-a-matter-of-factly assuming tone to it all. And I couldn't let that go. I couldn't. It was as if I had to defend logic itself, or else it might be swallowed whole by people like this.

"Then, they try to sell me on the idea of eternal life. Do these people even understand just how long that might be? Have they even considered the possibility that if something doesn't have an ending it could very well lose all meaning? I certainly don't want to live that long, and what would I even do with all that time? Life gets so unbearably dull, so dull. Most days, I end up having a nap because there's nothing else to do. Is eternal life supposed to be one never-ending party where we just eat, drink, and sleep endlessly? That's no heaven to me. That's hell. Really—what's life without the occasional thrill of your own mortality?"

The Drunk nodded along with understanding and without agenda. The Gambler held the floor.

"And I don't buy how God offers salvation for all. We're supposed to travel in his name to all the pagans and indigenous peoples of the world and spread his word. We get to Island X, let's say, and bring the glory of God to all its inhabitants, let's assume. Fantastic, although we were a little too late to save the village elder who died only a few hours before our ship landed. What a pity. What a pitiful old man whose soul is now lost forever. And a pity it is, then, for the other elders we happened to miss and the sickly child who we never had the chance to save as well. Gone are their souls into thin air or even burning in damnation for all I know. The same goes for the thousands perished before and all their

Chapter Five: Faith and Logic

ancestors, too. God never seemed to give them the opportunity that we so preciously have, being born in the right place at the right time.

"But anyways, that's enough. The whole idea behind faith gets my mind going. And I could just end the debate with one simple question: if two people hear the voice of God, which one is right? Both create the problem and then sell the solution. And of course, we are all sinners—the ultimate projection."

The Gambler placed his hands against the common room table as if he had exhausted himself from his own thoughts. He let out a small sigh in order to come to his senses. "So, you've been writing? How goes it?"

The Drunk sat stunned. An overwhelming transit of opinions and stances had come to a crashing silence. Convictions running seemingly as deep as a lifetime sucked the air out of the room, leaving none for play and pleasure. "Well, I'm not quite satisfied with it, but I do believe in it. It's a story not a great many know of, and I see it as a must to tell it as best as it can be told. So I spend all my days here looking for the right feeling behind each word. There's no other choice, really. It's simply what I must do."

"Then you are more hopeful than the last week. Good. Now, I was just thinking. I could use the cool air, and you've been bolted away in a room, writing all night. Why don't we go out to town for a quick walk and do a little window shopping?"

"It is a warm and beautiful day, yes, but I don't fare too well in public places. I'm afraid I could ruin your day, too. A similar thing has happened before. By the end, I was left clutching my head, unable to stop my mind from sending me more and more pain. Unease becomes anxiety and then that becomes heartache which then becomes loneliness and then panic, and it all ends in torrent. It would be unpleasant."

"Oh, that would be quite sad. So, then, I can't help but think of something: how is it, then, you are able to go to work around others in a factory when all that is true?"

"That's simple. When there is something I absolutely have to go do, then my anxieties know not to bother me. And I'll drink less before and after it, too, usually. For a short time, I cease to be what I am. For that time, I'm no longer a lone rat in a maze with only opium at its end, and the focus is on something much larger. Work is all powerful and sacred like that."

"All powerful and sacred? Do you believe in God, then?"

"I believe in forces stronger than myself, and it doesn't matter to me whether they come from God or elsewhere."

"Then we must find a force to get you out of this house."

"I'll let you know as soon as I find it," said The Drunk.

There was a brief lapse in the conversation as both fumbled about the impasse created.

"Do you know what causes all that anxiety?"

"That one is harder to explain. I'm not even sure words can ever describe it. But I can try.

"I like to think everyone has their heart's desire. Usually, it's a love interest, someone you pour all your hopes and dreams into and fantasize over the chance of gaining their attention, capturing their interest, and obtaining their love. For others, it is not a love interest that is our heart's desire but a vision or a need. And when that vision or need cannot be met, there is this unbearable pain. Some then say the source of all suffering is desire. And there was a time I thought I might join a Buddhist monastery somewhere far from here and spend the next 20 years ridding myself of all desires. But I realized, even if I did, it would all come back in some horrible, unknown single instant and be worse than ever, just like it has once before. Some things can be ignored for 20 years but not forever."

Chapter Five: Faith and Logic

"So what did you do instead?"

"For some of us, you can take a bright blue pill and have it take your desires with it, mostly."

"Interesting. That all makes sense except for one thing: if you still experience anxiety, then doesn't that mean you still experience desire as well?"

"Yes, but now it's an amount I can live with. Life is worth living again, and it is so, so sweet."

The Gambler held his eyes open and bobbed his head slightly with comprehension. He drew his next breath. "If you ever want some company around the house, you have me at least."

"I will gladly take you up on that offer. Let's have another feast sometime."

The Gambler bowed his way out of the common area with his morning cup, leaving The Drunk to tend to the cathedral made up of the Devil's water. It was then a craving struck, not for the scotch, rye, or bourbon assembled presently but for Irish whiskey instead, a rare occurrence. Their butterscotch, shortbread, and vanilla cream flavors delighted the many, but more often than not, they left a lingering grainy, metallic bitterness in the aftertaste for most. This day struck different, however. Such a drink was exactly what was desired.

A trip to the bottle shop then became a necessity. Where nerves usually rattled upon the thought of leaving the house, they were excited instead. The impending reward of more alcohol gave new movement to the body. Cheeks flushed with glee as if going to see old friends or meet potentially new ones.

Upon arriving, it was always rows of bottles to greet, not persons. The sight of them alone steadied the soul. Their labels were seductive and shameless; to read them was to flirt with them. Each and every bottle fought to entice the consumer and sell them on an image of the best possible evening. For many, their hearts were sold long ago to a single brand; others were open to variety as long as the price was right. The connoisseur, on the other hand, made advances towards all.

The game, then, was to lend one's imagination to distilleries, bottlers, and merchants and allow oneself to be sold. A winner was declared when one could not be without a certain bottle whether it was because its reputation, unique aging processes, or just the allure of the bottle design alone.

After an hour of tease and banter, a process of elimination would occur. Not all of them could be taken home. Some initially drew attention, yet a familiar feeling of deja vu would quickly disqualify them. Others were interesting enough to want to spend more time with, but there was no overwhelming spark of attraction. And several were reserved as maybes but for a later day.

Sometimes there were multiple winners, and one had no choice but to take them all home, such as now. The Drunk locked arms with new bottles and escorted them home.

There, conversations with friends new and old continued and soon became an impromptu gathering and party, unexpected to everyone. The Irish were welcomed with beckoning waves and come-hither looks by the bourbons and ryes, and they were made to feel appreciated just as the scotches once were. They told stories with their distinctive flavors that were truly one of a kind but yet rang true across all of humanity. The scotches then opened up and became emotional with their own tales made of joy, sorrow, and drams. Sensing the mood had begun to weigh down too far, the ryes joked about how unpopular they were with an undertone of true cheerfulness. And the bourbons made light of the fact that they'll both never see the day where they age past 30 years; the scotches looked away.

By the end of the night, as the sun was rising, the cocktail clatter had diminished into just a small number of voices, and

Chapter Five: Faith and Logic

periods of silence grew more and more frequent. Now was the perfect exit point for all remaining guests. The Drunk became too exhausted to go any further with those who persisted and stayed put and so said good night prematurely before retiring to bed for a deep slumber.

CHAPTER SIX:

SELF-ACCEPTANCE

The Drunk awoke that evening with an impressive amount of energy, considering the night before. To hope to be sharp and crisp at such a moment would be asking for too much, but to be functional was a luxury. The body could move, and so it did without even the slightest ache. There was no dread or apprehension about the upcoming long night of labor. An evening cup was savored in silence as earnest gratitude warmed the soul. Waking nightmares were a thing of the past and long since faded, and any day in their absence was a good one.

It was time for work. A pale and colorless meeting was adjourned. Menial roles and duties were assigned, upsetting several but never the calm and dignified. The belt burred and hummed into a start as laborers contemplated the end and all paths leading to it.

It was during the walk to the night's assigned post that a cold gust struck The Drunk from within. One person was now among one hundred. Conversation was abound all over, and connections were being made. New friends and even lovers were chatting for the first time or twentieth. But for The Drunk, where there was a

Chapter Six: Self-Acceptance

desire for connection, there were also unshakable, undeniable feelings of fraudulence. To present oneself was to tell a story, and The Drunk could present nothing but lies, lies to the self and others. Thoughts of being called out for such lies circled round and round and spiraled further into the mind. It begged for it, in fact, just so it could relieve itself through tears and go quiet once more. The anticipation could not stop itself.

Unlighted suspicions and impressions had mutated into a disturbed stirring that swept over The Drunk like a swift current. First, there were waves of isolation that caused the heart to retract into sadness. Then, its icy waters produced chills of loneliness. At last, a single thought pierced all sensation: it said, "Everyone is playing, and I cannot play." The next moment, the stunning beauty of a young girl came into view and passed before the eyes. A flurry of sorrowful emotions arose, and a torrent began.

A fellow laborer made haste towards The Drunk in an effort to console. Yet The Drunk's quaking lips could only blub in a language intelligible to one. Memories and memories flashed through the mind, not through images or events but by feeling alone. The contexts had long been forgotten, but their regrets resurfaced untouched, just as the day they were born.

The Drunk muffled a single phrase, yet the sound of whimpering overshadowed all meaning. The fellow laborer stood patient and on stand-by.

Tides began to calm, and speech could soon set sail again. It was then The Drunk saw the impotence of words in the face of what had just taken place. Describing the whole soul was the job of the poet and not a manual laborer. There was no use in saying anything meaningful or even coherent. Reducing the problem to an anxiety or a passing mood would be an insult to expression. And any type of reassurance would lead to a chain of obligated and half-hearted questions and answers. The only remaining option was to communicate a single truth. The lips parted.

"I cannot love a man."

Hours later, sorrow had quietly faded into a sedated calm. There was no zeal for work, yet all was stable once more. Fears had been realized, and their anxieties could now no longer harm The Drunk for the time being. All could flow as sparse rain droplets leisurely trickling down a glass pane. A calm soul need not anymore.

The last few minutes of labor counted down as always, and the clock finally gave way. Work had come to an end. The Drunk shuffled feet to the meeting place and awaited in silence. The Lover appeared in turn, and spirits became as warm as newly baked bread.

"You look beat today."

"I am. It's been an emotional day, for sure."

"How about I buy you a morning cup from somewhere nearby? And I do remember what you told me the other day about your struggles, so I have an idea this time."

"What's your idea?"

"I know a place that is opening in a quarter of an hour. It will be empty this early in the morning. There will be no one there. And there will even be an open rooftop where brick and sky will be all we can see."

The Drunk's face and eyes shot downward and away to a corner of the table. The lips were sealed when they were open and waiting to interject moments ago. There was no anxiety where there ought to be, for tears had already come to pass. In its place, there was a rare sobering stillness, a mild high that never lasted past a few hours. Suddenly, the idea of a morning cup never sounded as refreshing as now.

"I make no promises, but I'll go."

Chapter Six: Self-Acceptance

"Great. This is truly great. Follow me, and I'll take us there."

After a short commute, the two arrived and situated themselves with their drinks on the rooftop. All was empty as promised save for the hostess down the stairs.

"Look at that view," said The Drunk with curious eyes. "We can see the whole of downtown from here. That has to be at least a hundred buildings if we counted. I can't remember the last time I've seen such a thing."

"Yes, look at all of them. Many of those people have the same exact problem. We deal in the very same problem, too." The Lover's tone was now heavier than before.

"Oh, and what's that?"

"They cannot accept themselves. Instead, they play the victim, and it's always someone else who must answer. They must be treated a certain way, or the world is at fault. As you can likely guess, I am projecting here. Look at me. I'm five foot and some few inches tall. And I'm ugly as sin. I've even shaved off the littlest of hair on my head that was denying reality. But that's just it. I accept I am much more than what you see. I know this. I can feel it. I am alive with the energy women seek. It can be learned forwards and backwards."

The Drunk listened with a smirk that only grew with each passing word. The lips glowed with anticipation. Such a belief spoke directly to The Drunk's core being as dry tinder successfully kindles a fire. And how articulate were these ideas relayed and put forth, making way for such a delightful exchange to come. Passions brewed. The Drunk's gaze stood fixedly on The Lover's eyes all the while the beam across the face fattened and stretched.

"What? What are you grinning over there about?" The Lover asked, breaking into a soft laughter.

The Drunk sat there in silence, letting the grin speak for itself. It communicated play in a manner words never could. Words could argue, but an authentic smile never could.

"Why accept what you can change? I have a problem with all that you can see and many things you can't. If it can be changed, then I don't see why not. And if a surgeon can make you taller, I don't see why not either."

"No. And no. That would be cheating. Even if I did do it, it would cure a symptom but not its cause, which is on the inside. It would then follow me and become a new problem elsewhere, I'm sure of it. We must accept what we are, or we will never find joy in this life."

"Or the only things we must accept are the things we cannot change," The Drunk began. "To force anymore seems unnecessary or just mad. You know, every pure ideal has its shadow. Even love itself can become hate. And self-acceptance can become self-deception. Does that sound ridiculous? Maybe. Maybe so. But imagine you have a life you have struggled, truly struggled to keep and accept, after years of throwing it away or at least trying to, and from some darker than dark point, you bounce back into light and start to accept it and begin to make the best of it. Imagine then managing to build a career over 10 years, going from bitter tears to again taking you to the joys of childhood. From there, you have a business that you dedicate all of your time towards that gives your life purpose again and a sense that you are truly helping others. Imagine all of that. What a beautiful thing. And imagine all of that, the utter whole of it, one day not making you happy. None of it. And you wonder why. Why am I not happy? Why? Why? Then and only then it appears, the thought you thought once, and because it was so painful, you unknowingly vowed to never think it ever again. And there it is, suddenly. It's the idea that everything you've done in life is to hide from what you really wanted all along.

Chapter Six: Self-Acceptance

And after that, you will enter a place where there is no love where you cannot love. There, you will die. You will wish it so, and you will try to make it so. And your wish might very well come true. And if you do somehow manage to escape it, everything you once knew will remain there so that you can never deceive yourself again and experience the same horror twice."

The Drunk's lips contorted from emotion and closed tightly. The Lover's eyes responded, and no words were needed. There was a deep pause. It was a space best left undisturbed for the moment. At last, the air thinned out, and there was room to speak again.

"Wow, that is true adversity. You have grown so much from that I can see. That is what I would call fertile ground."

The Drunk's head then lifted from a place of self-reflection back into the immediate surroundings. Where there were empty furnishings, there were now a few parties enjoying their morning cups. But there was no unease. In its place, a groundedness stood firmly. Insecurities of mind seemed so far away at a moment like this.

"I don't recommend lying to yourself your whole life to get there," The Drunk said in a lighter tone. "So I wonder, then. If I wish to change so much about myself, will I always have something to be unhappy about? But to not change them, when it is possible, is just misery. It's no different than if I were to leave my house and sleep outside of it in the dead of an icy winter wrapped in bushy coats and covers. I would live, but why would I do that? Should we accept and struggle against all of nature, like Diogenes, and live in a giant urn out in the street? Can't you see? It's all just imaginary lines in the sand, and we're drawing them for other people in our heads every day."

"No. That's different. This is strictly about you and yourself. There lies the problem and the solution as well. But look, you spoke with heart earlier, and now you're talking from your head.

You feel it, right? There was a fire in your voice where there isn't anymore. It's been replaced with—dry air."

"Something does feel different now. I suppose you're right, yes. I don't want to bore you."

"Let's leave it at that, then. Look! Look at the beautiful women that have walked in for their morning cups. Their faces are not painted but yet attractive, and their outfits are simple but sweet. But— how are you feeling? Is everything alright?"

"It's so strange; I feel fine, surprisingly. I'm glad you're here with me. So—these girls—what do you think? Will one of them become your next date?" As The Drunk finished speaking, the day's earlier events flashed through the mind. An unseen wince followed.

"Maybe, but I don't date," said The Lover with a straight face. "If we go from one place to another and our clothes come off, then so be it."

"Then one day, yes? What until then?"

"Until then, I invite every girl I like with the loveliest of letters I can think up, and one will eventually come along. I know the best cafes, bars, and events happening throughout the whole city. Come with me next week, and I can show you more."

"I think I should, yes. This has been liberating for me, to say the least."

The usual conversation of specific books and literature then took place, and after all needing to be said was said, the two stood up, descended from the rooftop, and parted ways. While making way towards home, The Drunk recalled the last visit to that very same cafe.

It was 15 years ago. Nerves were strung upon entering. An immovable lump in the throat made the whole neck constrict when it came time to order. Infertile and barren words came out.

Chapter Six: Self-Acceptance

A fetching young girl standing behind feigned helplessness at the sight of her hand letting a coin fall to the floor. Wide and begging eyes beckoned a younger version of The Drunk for help, but the later became paralyzed. There was no use in wasting breath; any response would just be lying to the poor girl.

Sitting in a crowd with an afternoon cup in hand now, The Drunk was slipping into isolation. The face sank more with each passing moment. Where there ought to be stability, there was a sense of alienation.

The Drunk then reached for a sip of sealed water. Instantly, all anxieties were quenched. A warm hug was felt in the throat, followed by the stomach. The pain was beginning to subside, and the air grew blunt. A complex problem had found its simple solution. Another sip was necessary. And then another followed a minute later, followed by yet another the next. Finally, The Drunk was at last in harmony with all others around. The eyes took in the room once again, but where there ought to be tension, there was now a buttery peace. A crooked smile rose from the lips.

CHAPTER SEVEN:

PLAY TO PLAY

The next day, The Drunk had ample time while waiting to catch the right words for the biography in progress. Thoughts drifted to why and why again.

The writing itself felt rigid. It had to be done a particular way and no other. The rules were set. Evidence was to be collected and presented thusly. Any imagination would be met with doubt and scrutiny. There was feeling in the work, but it was compromised. It was to be always grounded in facts, which meant words could not fly.

For years, The Drunk had been in love with this type of work. It was a swift dance where words every so often leapt off the ground even if for a short time. The rules of the game had not changed since, but the sense of play had. The game was once open and free, and the objective was to keep it going by simply playing for the sake of play. Yet now, with enough time passing, it had become something quite entirely different, and the point of it all was to play to win. The game had been optimized, and the fun had been optimized out of it. Where others were content with playing

Chapter Seven: Play to Play

optimally for millions, The Drunk was not. A dream once dreamt night and day had become a reality as mundane as can be.

The Drunk was already on the third cup of coffee of the day. The first had been black, followed by one with a pinch of sugar. The third and current had been soured with milk and tasted of wetted wood. The fourth could only be saved by a splash of scotch.

Writing was yet to be done, so waiting was the only option. Wait for the end of the day to start drinking. Wait for the next line of the biography to appear. Wait for the idea for a novel to be conceived. Wait like a fisher for a peck from the rod. Wait like a dog for a signal from its master for play to begin.

Nothing could be more lively than play, true play. That type of play would never waste your time. After a full day of work, a mild satisfaction might fill you and hold you for the evening; yet after a day of childlike play, you would always be left with the knowledge of a well-lived life.

It was then The Gambler entered the common room where The Drunk was absent-mindedly staring at paper, lost in another world.

"I see the writing is pouring from your soul as usual."

The Drunk smiled brightly, saying nothing at first, and then opened the mouth as if to speak until words could be found. "Sure, yes. Tell me, do you have a favorite story from your time at the casino. I seem to be low on stories at the moment."

"Well, let's see. Ah, there's always the beggar at every casino making his rounds asking for a dollar. You fall for that once before you see them deposit it right back into the slot machine."

"Do you play the slots?"

"Not anymore, no. One day, I was passing the night away at one of the penny machines. I had never won anything large from them, but it's perfect when you are low on everything except time. I must have played for countless hours that night when all at once every bell and whistle this machine had rang and blew. Lights all around were flashing and dimming, knocking me out of my waking sleep by downright blinding me. It was so loud and fierce that I was sure someone would come, so I looked around but saw no one. All there was to do was to wait until the machine released my winnings. I started to think of all the debt I could repay and how I could turn my whole life around, and then lo and behold, out comes $13.80. A grand total of $13.80. All this—excitement—everything for $13.80. Every emotion I had was manipulated, and I didn't even take the money out of—hatred and spite. I left it right there I was so mad. And it still makes me mad just thinking about it."

The Drunk sat stunned in silence. The Gambler shook his head over and over in disbelief and abruptly threw his arms in the air, as to discard his anger. The moment passed.

"Is it true there are no clocks inside at all?"

"Of course. Casinos are very, very clever in keeping you inside for as long as possible. Seeing the time puts you in your head where thinking then starts. I know their schemes all too well, and yes, they absolutely work. You may be too smart for them, yet they got me with a ball and chain. I get hotel reservations on the house from them all the time. It's all been calculated; they know how much I'm worth to them. And in the end, I get got. The odds are always in their favor; that is their business."

The Gambler paused briefly as his face lowered and a smile breached his face. An impish tint could be seen at the top of his eyes. "Now, there is one game you can take those odds back into your favor, not from other players but from them: and that is not poker but blackjack.

"Normally, most players join a table to throw their money here and there, have a drink or three, and enjoy the waves of emotions that come with each hand. Some win; most lose to the house,

Chapter Seven: Play to Play

however. But now, see here, what if an apt and sober player were to precisely count each card played so that they might better predict the cards not yet played? Such a thing is not only true but I happen to have been ousted from many casinos for doing so. What I did was perfectly in tune with the game and its rules, but these casinos will claim I have cheated them. Yet what cheating is there in just calculating your best moves? It sounds to me that someone doesn't want to share their ill-gotten gains and fortunes. They are capitalists, but so am I. And what could be more capitalist than to find a competitive advantage and to wring it for all its worth?"

The Drunk's eyes widened with wonder. It was almost as if to better peer into a world not yet known. In that world, there were flickers from a past life where brain and intellect were once the guiding forces day to day.

"Wow. And were you successful in making your money?"

"Thousands. I'm up quite a bit as of recent. Over a lifetime, however, that's not exactly the case. Give me a year of card counting, and I may recover what I lost and maybe even a bit more."

"Did you lose that money through blackjack?"

"Not exclusively, no. But I've only just begun to count. And even now, after six, seven, eight hours of counting or poker, I'll be exhausted, and I'll go make some—very dumb decisions," The Gambler said with hesitation.

"Dumb decisions? Which kind?"

"I don't know. I'll just be there making the same mistakes again and again, never learning and instead just betting more and more, chasing after my losses, only to go further and further into a darker than darker place. Or yet, I'll find myself throwing money away at roulette or, even worse, rolling it away with dice. It's embarrassing really, especially when you know better. I tell only you, though."

"I don't think that's very dumb at all. It makes perfect sense, in fact."

"It's pretty dumb, trust me."

"You want the game to continue, right? So you play to keep the game going for as long as possible. And you don't want to think, and you don't want to sleep."

"Maybe. What makes you say that?" The Gambler's eyes curled with questions.

"Because I think I'm the same: each glass can be like a new hand of poker. And while we're here, let me make another guess. It's not about winning, I think; it's about play, and there's something—naughty about it."

"It's not about winning, yes. It's about not knowing if you will win or not. That's the thrill of it all. But with blackjack and poker, it is more so about winning. It's so, so satisfying to watch your hard work and patience pay off after hours of play. There, I can win it all back with enough time. I just need to leave while I'm ahead."

The Drunk nodded along to The Gambler's words, however, with nothing further to say. To go any further was to soil hopes and dreams. And to soil them was to soil the chance of gaining control over one's own vices. Any hope was a good hope.

"What are you thinking just now?" asked The Gambler. "Your mind went somewhere else."

"Oh, I only wish I was as reassuring as you are. If I were to say anymore, I would be projecting my own lack of control."

"What do you mean by that? Tell me."

"Then I will tell you," The Drunk said and then paused to gather thoughts. A moment passed.

"It's a cycle. Do you see it? It's this cycle of pain and pleasure, and it starts with one or the other. You know, I've taken many breaks from drinking now and even quit once, yet I've always come back.

Chapter Seven: Play to Play

"There is a genuine love and passion I have for drinking, not beer, wine, rum, or vodka but whiskey. If it's not art, it's the closest thing to it. And every great bottle has a story to tell. There's a history and science behind every famous distillery, and they all have their unique smells and distinct tastes.

"So I come back to it one night or another, and it's only two glasses I'll want. And it's delicious. I may only ever want two glasses this night and that night for however long it lasts. Then, it's not tolerance I feel grow as time goes by but desire. And it grows, and it grows and grows. And one day, it will meet some unresolved pain or fear. There, it will nestle itself and make a home. And from that point, that desire has outgrown me and become its own person with its own voice. And then, all I can do is give it what it wants until it hurts me again. And every drop will be delicious."

The Gambler stood with eyes fixed on a wall, lost in thought. There was no initial response. Finally, the way forward appeared in front of him.

"You're right. You really shouldn't have said anymore." The room filled with contagious bits of laughter, and tensions were relieved.

"In all fairness, I do need a break from gambling. It's distracted me from my work, and it shows. My sales have been down all month, which has made a certain somebody quite upset with me. I haven't enough to be able to quit, but oh, do I wish it. To the devil with insurance. Almost everything about it makes me think of crying children."

"Then, after everything, you're still the one in control?"

"For now, I would say so. Card counting and poker are true trades, and hundreds have made their fortunes doing so. That is the dream, not working for some—muttonhead."

"Me neither."

"That's right. You will write that prizewinner one of these days, right?"

"You know, if I sold out to one political party or the other and wrote something cleverer than clever, people would pay a good deal of money for that sort of thing. But I can't. I just can't. There is no nuance in that world, and I would hate it, especially for the story I want to tell."

A mild pause came between the two.

"There is something about this biography I believe in even if it takes me the whole next year to write. Until then, I drink. You gamble. Maybe in moderation. Maybe a bit more. Somewhere along the line we start to like it a little bit too much. I started drinking because I wanted to take the edge off, you know. But what exactly was 'the edge'? What about it made me not want to sit with it? It didn't terrify me, but I didn't want it around. Then, years later, tragedy strikes, and suddenly then, all I could see was terror. Sorry. I'm repeating myself now; I've been looking forward to a glass all day. Give me one, just one, and you'll hear no more."

"It's about that time I see."

It was then The Drunk retracted and retreated into seclusion to retire for the night. Writing no longer mattered. Being sober no longer mattered. The brain could no longer distract with its puzzles and games and was next to useless at this hour, or so it was told.

The aches and pains of a liquored soul were now fully exposed.

Sitting at a desk in private, The Drunk lie in wait as agitation pecked through a thinning willpower and nibbled at the softest places in the mind. The brow stretched up and down as far as it could in hopes of escaping anxiety altogether, yet it failed. The room itself offered no sympathy or comfort and seemed to laugh at every wince and shake. There was no reason to go for a walk when it would only prolong thirst and cause it to be greater at the finish than at the start. And reading was long out of the question.

Chapter Seven: Play to Play

It was time. A morsel of food was downed and immediately followed the bottle. Glasses would come later. There was relief, instant relief, mingled with vague rye whiskey flavors. With a squint of the eyes, there was mint, oak, licorice, cherry, and spices that lingered in the throat.

For a moment, they stayed, yet in the next, they were beginning to fade. Never had whiskey flavors come and gone so quickly before, and their absence was felt at once as a deeply disturbing reality.

Perhaps a glass was necessary, then, and so the second whiskey, a Speyside scotch, was poured without delay. Normally, there would be a customary ten minute wait to allow all flavors to open up, although this particular scotch The Drunk had already experienced again and again. The glass was twirled and twirled; the wait, however, could not wait. It was bottomed. And it was pure goodness. Malt, pears, grapes, pepper, smoke, charred barrel, must, and sour funk had all melded into one thing.

Wincing and shaking had been replaced by sinking and rolling. Anxiety become diluted and then was flushed out completely.

Minutes later, the scotch, too, was dissipating. A second glass was brought forth, and a classic Irish whiskey soon filled it. A few swirls, a tipping and turning to coat the glass, and even a sniff took place. Only alcohol could be discerned after giving the glass a mere seconds to breathe. Waiting was over. The glass was downed. Buttery vanilla and many other notes were all there, for sure, but moreso, its goodness overtook all. For if this was not good, nothing was. Writing was good, and work was good; but without this, it was all meaningless. The day had lead to this moment again and again. Work was a means to make play all the sweeter.

The bottles had never looked more beautiful. A barrel-strength bourbon was grabbed by the handle. Its corked popped, and a swig was taken. There was no flavor but one, and it was good, so good.

The numbness of the head grew too heavy to hold and thus tilted back while already reclining in the chair. Everything was better like this, yet none of it mattered; only this mattered. It was a true connection that could be found nowhere else but here and now. There was nothing to smile about, which had made The Drunk's smile even brighter. There was a joke somewhere that no one else could hear; however, it needed no words and was funnier without them. The evening now glowed just as the morning had while the head bowed and bounced compulsively.

The Drunk resigned there with content for some time until its absence could be felt. This time, a Texan whiskey made its appearance, and its charm was like no other in the room. The heart was quickly won over, and the bottle was uncorked. Two gulps worth was taken with ease, and two more could easily have followed. It tasted of a full-length, broiling Texan summer distilled into a single moment, and it was more than good. The mouth seared with extreme heat and oak, and words seemed to come forth from it. But they were unintelligible.

Play was coming to an end. There were no winners or losers. The game was instead kept alive for as long as possible, yet now its players were all ready to turn in. The Drunk collapsed onto the bed with thoughts of play to resume tomorrow.

CHAPTER EIGHT:

THE PAINTING AND THE MACHINE

The laborers had made it to lunchtime at the factory. Menial tasks were therapeutic in their proper amount, but the dosage had been set far too high. Famished and demoralized faces made way to a special luncheon prepared. It was not food they wanted, but food was taken, while a bitter hunger for higher salaries remained. Morale did not seem to improve or worsen.

But today was such a special occasion that The Drunk had been invited to join a table to dine with the most open and vocalized group in the room. For weeks, The Drunk had heard much laughter and joy from this party, even while often sitting at the opposite corner of the very same dining hall. There was an envious desire to take part in this crowd, for outside of it, the room was an empty void of tables lined with those who would quite rather have been somewhere else.

Conversation floated between all members of the party. At one moment, one person could be speaking with solely one other, and in the next, they could address the whole with a stark observation all could easily see and understand.

Banter was the thread to connect them all. It was a game of wits and to touch the line but never to cross it. Everyone who participated was fair game as well. Even those who did not speak joined in by lending their ears, which in turn, added to the value of all words exchanged.

Soon, the quipping softened, and the group broke off entirely into waves of smaller exchanges for the time being. The Drunk was in the thick of six to seven conversations all converging into a harmony of warm souls and spirits. One such pair were discussing rising costs of living in the inner city. Another were sharing corpulent, corn-fed dreams of salt, fat, and sugar taken to their extremes. There were, then, the three making their family affairs public with an air of moderate importance. And of course, there was talk somewhere of the latest shows and theater, this time coupled with how it was nothing compared to what it once was.

It would be too easy to label all of it as light and mundane, for even the most cynical would be lying if they said they could not feel any heart or sincerity at all. At their core, these were mostly ordinary folks but occupied in an intense struggle for survival. Not a thing else had a place when one's livelihood and sense of inner stability were at constant odds with the world around them.

And so, The Drunk could only but listen. Bookish talks of finding meaning or of literature would be heard by no one. Faces would only contort with mild aversion. And it was next to useless to talk of problems no other could relate to; The Lover would not appear until the second half of the long night.

The cafeteria chatter continued. No one batted an eye towards The Drunk, who sat very reservedly with hands folded in the lap and eyes fixed at a distance away. And this was good. Even better was the unexpected level of peace while among so many. With that,

Chapter Eight: The Painting and the Machine

a need for human interaction was oddly met, for life was grand enough.

As the special luncheon concluded, work soon resumed. The well-fed laborers carried themselves back to their stations with indifference and ingratitude. Morale was just as it had been.

A number of hours passed in a stupor, and it was time to return home. The Lover emerged from the crowd of the common while The Drunk awaited at the usual rendezvous. Eyes met. Mouths opened.

"Today, we are going to another cafe. You'll like this one, trust me. Follow me."

The Drunk's brow twitched upward, and lashes flickered twice.

The two made way downtown where culture and commerce intersected. There, at the cafe, aesthetic was present, accompanied by equally elaborate pricing. Certainly, though, class and elegance could be seen and felt, which seemed to justify it all.

The Drunk and The Lover seated themselves among the morning crowd.

"How do you feel?" The Lover asked.

"Calm, and it's been a long time since I felt that in a place like this. But we are in our own space here, so nothing else matters."

"OK. Now, look around this room. There's so much life in this very room, and they willingly choose to waste it for work. To slave away their youth, for what? For a mortgage? To stuff a large and empty house with as much fluff as they don't need? To appease their wife and children who lost respect for them years ago? For comfort? To be comfortable and then die? What a waste of life."

"You lump them all into the same category? How can you be so sure?"

"Look at them again. Their bodies are static. Their faces are soulless."

"That's because they're working. And it's a beautiful thing, a holy thing."

"They came all the way here to do that? I don't believe it."

"I can. A writer needs fire, and there's a spark hiding about here."

The Lover looked around once more out of disdain. His brow furrowed with disapproval. The Drunk took in a few more glances as well.

"These men are so effeminate, and I can't stand it. They're perched like birds, as to say, 'Look at me! Come up to me! I am too much like a woman to do so, so come to me, please!' It's disgusting. Where is their masculinity? Why do they hide it? Have they let this world castrate them and turn them into asexuals?"

"I think they may have heard that."

"As they should. They need it. Excuse me for a moment."

The Lover abruptly stood up with a momentum that carried more by the second. He strode past a number of gentlemen seated gingerly with their candied papers. No one dared to turn their head. He then arrived at the bar counter to greet the maiden there, a very young and stunning doll. Her golden braids and blushed face made it tempting to stay for more than just tea. She smiled and reciprocated The Lover's warm gestures and invitations. His arms were swollen with pride and might, and he had even seemingly grown five inches taller.

After a brief exchange lasting mere seconds, The Lover returned and reclaimed his seat.

"Lovely lady she was. She deserved to know that much."

"I think she may already know."

"But she was in her head, going about her usual day. Who knows what kind of insecurities and doubts take hold of her mind? And a single kind word melts it all away. And now, this day has become a good one."

Chapter Eight: The Painting and the Machine

"Why not go on with her more? I don't mind."

"That will come later. But do you see it? I know your struggles with your face and other things, yet none of this truly matters. You are your own tormentor, and you willingly whip yourself, you know; you have the power to stop it any time you choose. Do you know how? It's simple. Thinking is a disease, and the heart is the cure."

"This is true. Yes, you're right. But only is it true when I am alone. It is only then I feel everything you say and more. It will be in the morning usually. I'll make a cup and go to my desk to hang my head to dream while awake. I'll pick a spot. That spot on the floor will do, and it's always that spot my eyes go to and stop at. And there will be no thoughts. There will be no need for thoughts. There will be no problems to solve. All will seem to have been said and done. Desires don't exist then. If there were any desires, there would be thoughts, then, which there are neither. And when there are no desires or thoughts, there is this bliss instead, and I sit with it. Is it happiness? I don't think so. I'm not sure what it is, but it's there every day I choose. It doesn't last forever, but for one, two, three, and sometimes even five hours, it can go on. And it will end, and when it does so, there will then be both thoughts and desires; so work begins and so do my problems."

The Lover's hands and eyes were utterly focused in delivering a response. They slightly and slowly raised then fell at once.

"That which you just described to me you can have here and now. If you would only ignore your self-conscious thoughts and doubts and instead embrace everything you are right now, you could overcome it all."

"For what? False connections to a false person? None of it would feel real; none of it would *be* real. They would see me for something I am not. They would never see me no matter what.

And it would only hurt. And at that point, I am no longer there then and cannot be with them."

"I disagree but fine. Just don't go around writing self-empathy sob story garbage. It's bad art. But anyways, look over there. Do you see that couple? Yes, right there. Finally, two people who actually look alive. Look at them move. All that movement even while seated. The man—he leans in and out with complete control over himself and the conversation. You can see his face is locked on to hers, and he's so calm and composed; he's waiting for the perfect opportunity to strike. Look at how she crosses her legs but draws closer when he speaks. Do you see it? Do you see how her eyes and hips move with him wherever he goes? One moves away as the other draws closer all while she teases him at every turn. There's a tension between them, and it's playful. Every word has emotion in it, always building, one after the other. It's language, but there's no logic and reason to it, only rhythm. Can't you feel that? That there is the most beautiful thing in the entire world."

As The Lover was depicting the scene, The Drunk's face grew more and more distressed. Every word said was true. It was a language, although it was foreign. And it could be translated into English, but it could not be felt. What was natural and even primal to The Lover and this couple and the world was a cold and lonely silence to The Drunk. It all made sense and could be studied and learned, like a science, but never felt.

The woman was undoubtedly very attractive yet attractive as far as a painting could be to The Drunk. The eyes feasted, but touch would render nothing.

The man had as much charm and seductiveness and handsomeness as a machine could. He was functional, well-maintained, and effective when needed; there was, however, no need or desire for him.

Everything that should be there was there not at all.

Chapter Eight: The Painting and the Machine

A familiar aloneness took hold of The Drunk. Where there was a radiant smile moments ago, there were now drooping lips. All persons instantaneously became a source of immense discomfort. The Drunk's innards recoiled away from all and towards the emptiest corner of the room. The heart raced, and a pressing need to go where it was both dark and solitary seized the mind. Words were beginning to fail.

"What's wrong? Tell me."

"I can't. I have to go. I'm sorry."

The Drunk took flight and fled directly home. Along the way, melancholy became wrath. Tears became exhaustion. Quietness became disconnection. And, in the end, there was nothing left but a puncture in the spirit and a restless soul.

An irresistible desire for satisfaction flooded the mind and the heart. To acknowledge it was the best revenge.

The door home opened and shut. Shoes came off and onto the rack. A cabinet door slid left then right. A cork was popped and popped.

Stubborn laughter filled the halls of the empty house, followed by nervous snickering. A deep breath only now became natural to take. Relief flushed across the cheeks at an unnatural rate, which soon spread to the lips, causing a very pleasant tingle and a spoiled smile in turn before reaching the forehead, the epicenter of today's madness and tomorrow's rationality. And the numbing was good.

The mind had gone on an awful rampage and had lost its privileges for the day. Its thoughts were not The Drunk's but instead a rowdy neighbor upstairs that required the occasional appeasement.

It was then the idea to have a meal came to mind. There was no appetite, but the swelling liver called out for it. A melody started to accompany the hands and feet while plates pattered and broccoli browned from heat. And the mood was light again.

A warm embrace could be felt, and it asked for no returning affection. All was connected once more.

The moment was ripe for reflection. Years ago, off in a far distant country in Asia, The Drunk spent the evening with an old friend who was visiting. Tucked away in a mostly unlit corner of a sprawling city, there lay a row of miniature taverns, each able to seat only four or five at a time. Seating was intimate, and so were the conversations that occupied them.

The two longtime friends had years of stories to catch up on as they jumped from tavern to tavern. They talked of language and travel as well as truth and longings, relived memories through retellings and laughter, and heartily reconnected during many moments throughout the night.

Then, at a certain point, an unforgettable one, the old friend ordered a top shelf drink for the occasion. Never had The Drunk ever seen a barman climb a ladder so high for any drink. The thought to spend so lavishly on something temporal and fleeting seemed absurd when it could go towards a much greater cause.

The bottle itself was dressed in a plain label, and for that reason, it was bold. It held so much confidence in its essence that it required little else.

An untraveled American would clench their teeth, turn their nose, and take pleasure in their repulsion just at the mention of the word *scotch*, but a common Englander would perk up a naughty smile, fully knowing what was just poured into their glass.

The Drunk raised the glass curiously and gave it a whiff. Inside was the most pristine and distinct smell a soul could ever encounter in a lifetime. The mind fell inward and traveled in a direction new and unfamiliar to parts not quite known. It moved downward and deeper but was unable to latch onto any tangible memory and instead hit upon some past feeling of a true self not felt in a very long time.

Chapter Eight: The Painting and the Machine

The night had come to a mystic halt with a single truth. And it had begun to vanish no later than it had arrived. And yet it was more real than anything that came before or after that day and night. All else was lying in some shape or form.

The Drunk was certainly seated with an old friend. Passion and love had been there with every word spoken and each step taken. That could not be denied. But underneath it all, lay something far more meaningful, and no trace of it now remained.

Like a dream where one is on the verge of solving the great mystery of one's life, the soul reaches out to touch and grasp the solution to it all and immediately finds itself waking up with empty hands and only the faintest idea of the truth.

All else that night in the faraway land quickly faded into nothingness, and the remainder of the present day would soon do just the same.

CHAPTER NINE:

THE EMPYTY GLASS

The Drunk awoke the next day with slow and soggy eyes. The body lay still for some time, gratified with itself. The day could wait, for the moment was already full with a defiant glee. There were no people to see, places to go, or things to do; or in other words, it was to be a good day.

Eventually, the thought for a morning cup pressed and pressed again, and the feet started. Upon heating and pouring, the writing desk and chair were sought for more stillness.

To sit with peace once again rendered time and all else unnecessary. The common clock on the white wall was amusing alone; every minute ticking by was followed by another to enjoy. The frivolous dreamer knew better than to work and so safely ignored thoughts of writing, if only for a passing time. There and then, in this space, it was obvious that nothing mattered, which brought relief and rest for the time being.

The room would laugh, and it was contagious. Worries would lazily fly about and latch onto the cup and be gone with a sip. Books piled on the desk made it possible to have conversations with friends who lived hundreds of years ago and who also would

Chapter Nine: The Empty Glass

never leave. Yet these were friends who asked for one's full attention, and if anything was to be attended now, it would be work.

It was this last thought that seeped into the background and waited around. It could not be laughed off or sipped away.

The common clock on the white wall even seemed to gain new meaning, for time was no longer ticking up but down. The body gently rocked with slowly rising speed while the room laughed no more. Peace saw itself out the door as a noisy mind began its usual chattering of lofty ideas. An uneasy hand reached for pen and pad.

There was then but one problem: it had been weeks since any true progress had been made on the biography. Its flow had completely dried up with its crinkled papers now resembling a cracked soil.

There was resistance, and The Drunk questioned why. It would, in all likelihood, be a success, and all its pieces were at hand, ready to be assembled. They simply needed to be laid together brick by brick, and once done so, the ending result would be worth it in ways more than one.

The story had been composed in such a way to give everything the people wanted. It was a study of many best-selling works that came before it and was built to last into the unknowable future. Themes and characters were thoughtfully designed around a proven recipe. There was just enough originality to be interesting and enough safety to be prosperous.

And yet the story had no living pulse.

There was nothing to carry it through the bog every work must travel through. It was not the first days, weeks, or months that tested a creator's resolve, nor was it the final stages either; it was always the middle where hopes and aspiring creations would live or die based on solely one thing: its irrational stubbornness to exist. Where there was a crisis, adrenaline could carry any work through any difficulty, but where there was no crisis, belief would carry an idea only as far as it was meaningful. And The Drunk was now out of both adrenaline and belief.

Still, there was a joy to be found even in death. Every creation hummed and drummed to its own beat from its first till its last. Each was a newborn that was wowed by every little new thing in a world full of little new things. Eventually, every tune and melody goes quiet, and every lucky child grows old; and its original spirit is no more. In its place, that same spirit finds itself in a new body, entirely unsure of how it got there.

The joy of creation had long existed in The Drunk before any crisis and any weariness, and only now, could it be seen again.

It had awakened once more.

Pure passion descended into the room, untamed and without form, powerful but without words. It was a story waiting to be captured, but how to do so was a mystery and a puzzle and a secret.

Both fueled and famished after a journey of ideas, The Drunk laid pen and pad down and headed to the common room for another cup. There, The Gambler was standing with the same exact craving.

"Well, well, well, is it time for whiskey already? I never know with you and your—kind of schedule."

"I'll take a morning coffee, but how about a whiskey later together, too? It's been a wonderful day, and I have so much to tell you about."

"Of course. What happened?"

"Tonight, I will tell you." Soon after, The Drunk took a hearty coffee back up the stairs and continued to gather thoughts and conjure up new ones.

Hours then passed, and it was evening. The Gambler had prepared a voracious spread as per usual in his private room. Those who say gluttony is akin to filling a bottomless pit simply have

Chapter Nine: The Empty Glass

never dined with one who knows how to eat. The same may be said of alcohol, for The Drunk had lined the table with some of the finest bourbon, rye, and scotch money could buy. Greed itself smiled at such a gathering.

"I'm sorry for leaving so quickly earlier. There was a breakthrough, and it came at the time I least expected it to."

"You finished the book?"

"No. That's just it. I won't finish it. I don't even need to anymore because I found an even better one to write. But I haven't really *found* it. I felt it. And—there it was again like a child who is ready to play again after falling down. You know—it was never about the money from the start. Every child is smart enough to know that. And we were never taught it, but we forget. We were taught to forget it. And then one day, it was about nothing but money. And unhappiness. It's that 'one day,' though. *That* is the story. But—how could I ever make sense of it? Who would ever understand it? You would never be able to feel it."

"I'll try. Tell me."

"That's just the thing. I don't think I can, not like this anyways. But—I have an idea. I want to ask you something. Do you—believe in demons?"

"No, of course not. That's usually something people use to scare me into joining their stupid holy book club. I like books, but does it really have to be the same book week after week? Can't we—but anyways, go on."

"You told me the other day about those who talk of the end days. Remind me of what you said exactly."

"It's almost always the ones poor in health and past the age of 50 who talk about it. They're close to the end, and they project that onto others wherever they go."

"Yes, what do you call that? Projection?"

"I wouldn't call it no demon, for sure."

"What do you call it when you gamble?"

"Gambling," The Gambler said with a fat smile while The Drunk's eyes rolled.

"The point is you told me your end goal. You will beat the casino at its own game and all in the open and fairly. But have you ever thought about why it means so much to you?"

"I would say learning a strategy and watching it pay off is addictive, but I know that's not what you mean. Then, if you ask and if I think, if I were to guess, it might be because of what I was given. Maybe it's because I was given so much, all from a family that never asked for much in return. Truly, I couldn't have asked for anymore. I was allowed to try anything I wanted, but I was also allowed to give up at anytime I wanted. So I did. These things, education, opportunity, all these things, meant nothing to me. They were given to me, but I never asked for them. And now, they've all gone to waste. My parents are great, truly great people, and I'm afraid I've done nothing but disappoint them. So, is this what you mean?"

"Yes. Go on. Why gambling?"

"Because it's addictive, and yes, that is exactly why it's the one thing I don't want to give up on. It's not as simple as watching the roulette ball and hoping it lands on gold. No, that's an idiot's game. The only thing dumber than that is rolling dice where your chances are at the lowest. It's blackjack and poker that can be learned, that can be studied, that can be conquered. It's that hit from outsmarting a person and profiting off of them. That there is the dream. I was given this brain that I never asked for, and there, I've found the one way to keep it occupied—and safe."

There was a long pause.

"Let's drink to gambling, then," The Drunk said with a roguish look.

Chapter Nine: The Empty Glass

Glasses came forth, and bottles clanged as hands reached for a special dram. Hidden behind the bourbons, ryes, and scotches was a Japanese whiskey, which now rested at the center of the spread. Its bottle design was so ornate and grandiose that all who were offered it might guess they were in for a high-class treat.

"I don't bring out this one very often, you know."

"That's what they all say. But yes, that is one very nice-looking bottle."

"And what's inside is even better. I'd love to hear what you think about this one."

Two glasses were poured.

"And now we wait for it to open up a bit. It needs just a few minutes before its flavors are at their fullest like any good wine."

"How about some poker?" asked The Gambler with a slight twist in the lips.

"I don't know how to play."

"Okay, then. I will teach you. I'll show you my world as you've shown me yours."

A telescreen blinked on. On it, there played a broadcast of a high-stakes poker match. The Gambler explained who the top players were and how they were exactly able to extract all the money from the lower-level players at the table. There were bluffs and calling of bluffs, but the best were so calculated that they could accurately predict the average player's style of play within just a few minutes. From there, they could read every hand that player was dealt and know just when and how much to wager to get the most money out of them. A true professional could reduce people to keys to be played on the piano.

The two watched a few hands play out in real time. The Drunk glanced over at The Gambler, who seemed to have fallen into a daydream. His eyes were locked and engaged, but his mouth was gaping in stupor. Surely, he was here in the room, but clearly, he had gone somewhere else; and wherever he had gone to, appearances did not matter.

A world of intellect, analysis, and numbers had no concern for all else. Winning was done by the book, and all the fun was in playing closest to its rules. There was no room for banter or jokes in the face of what mattered most. Any misplay was internally chastised on the spot by all serious players observing, while the professionals were treated as lions among sheep, free to eat whoever happened to be their next victim. Over time, these players had built a society made up of minds and perspiration, which thrived on the perverse enjoyment of flogging oneself and promises to do better.

The Drunk had seen this world somewhere before in a past lifetime. It was completely foreign now. Almost unreal was it then to look at with new eyes. Good or bad could not be seen in this world, but there was a glimpse into the goodness of humanity coming to terms with all that was bad in the world. It was the work of ego doing what it does best, which was to survive.

On the surface, there was a game, yet it had been played so much that it had become something altogether different. Play had been perfected; its spirit was the cost. And The Gambler loved it.

A long round of poker on the telescreen had concluded.

"The whiskey should be ready by now," said The Drunk.

"You go first, then. This next hand could be it."

A glass was picked up. Its smell pierced the nose despite still being so far away. It was sweet like a smoking honey, and The Drunk's head tilted back with cheeks absolutely brimming.

The nose approached the whiskey. There was malt, candied melons, figgy plums, and a hint of spices while oak lingered beneath them all, coming and going at whim. Everything was light and floral, and nothing was in the extreme. All were touches from a

Chapter Nine: The Empty Glass

broad range of flavors, including citrus and grain, designed not to impress but to cause wonder.

A large sip was taken. The Drunk's head rattled backwards, shaking with every sensation ticking one after another. The eyes flinched shut with thoughts of buttery vanilla and cream. Tastes of glazed lemons contorted the face one way; images of stewed fruit twisted it another. The eyes shot open with a firm belief that something could be both musty and delicious. And it all finished with a glow of salt and ginger in the throat.

"Seeing that face will never grow old."

"But only if you knew, you would know."

"Alright. Let's see what's causing all the commotion."

The Gambler picked up his glass and gave it a thorough sniffing. Eyes seemed to be searching for the right words and settled into position for a short-lived time before returning to the game at hand on the telescreen.

"Smell anything?"

"Not sure."

While the match continued, The Drunk finished off the first glass with gratitude. A contented burst of air came forth from the lips and a muffled moan followed. Without delay, a second whiskey, a Highland scotch, was poured.

The latest round of poker ended, and once again, The Gambler made a reappearance in full. Without a word, he brought the drink back under his nose again; an inspection took place accompanied by a judge's impartial gaze. The glass turned up, and the liquid slipped down. A pulse could be seen making its way across the brows. While his jaw began to descend in order to make words, a distant stare was searching for language located far away. Eyes blinked.

"It's very smooth."

"Oh. Anything else?"

"I don't think so. What am I supposed to taste?"

"Only what you taste. But how about this? The first smell I got from it was almost like a smoked pineapple. See if you can find that."

"I'll give it a go, then. Well, now that you've said so and I smelled it again, I see what you mean. But just a moment. The next hand is starting."

The Gambler's vacant state resumed at once. The Drunk tended to the room with thoughts alone. Two different worlds appeared to occupy the same space. It was not cold or unmannered but the ultimate reality between any two souls.

Laid before The Drunk was a full glass and an empty glass. A vague idea emerged, and the head churned it round and round in hopes to make it smooth as butter. An overflowing glass could be seen through contagious pride and joy and thus shared with others; an empty glass could be seen through a miserable face but never shared, for there was nothing to share to begin with. When a person did try to share an empty glass with others and describe their sufferings, the words could be understood, but they pointed to something that could not truly be seen or felt without experience. To intellectualize suffering, to build a monument to it, these were no better. To paint hell as it was, however, this could at least be made beautiful, but there was something more, a point far beyond it all to reach. A new thought then appeared: joy was universal; misery was personal.

In the next moment, it was The Drunk who returned to the room, now exhausted after a spell of thinking. A full glass was bottomed, and the soul was instantly replenished with a sweet and sour wholesomeness. Life swam with flavor and intensity again, lasting for minute after minute with a lingering richness that hugged the throat and echoed oak and beauty. By the end, it was merely the beginning as there were still several glasses left to

Chapter Nine: The Empty Glass

consume. Soon, a comforting thirsty haze came rushing forth to seal the night away.

CHAPTER TEN:

A STRANGER IN A VOID

T he Drunk fully awoke at the warehouse the following day. The familiar blur of fatigue and numbed emotions had ended at its usual hour but was replaced this time by something blackhearted.

Conscious insights and their pains had been fully restored, and they could not help but direct themselves towards a disconnected reality. People, here or there, in a factory or in a concert hall, in an uptown cafe or in an open park, could be nothing more than people, each with their own desires, going about endlessly fulfilling them. Conversations with friends new and old were initially full of joy and laughter before devolving with the eventual truth of people's most basic nature, killing all curiosity and wonder and possibilities for surprises. And romance was a transaction between two warm bodies in a marketplace of flesh. Without the illusion of love, people were nothing but a list of desires to be transacted and bodies to be obligated.

Thoughts turned inward, seeking resolution, but could not find any.

Chapter Ten: A Stranger in a Void

The face immediately went pale, and the feet grew cold. Labor was ongoing. A pitiful step was taken as the body heavily turned to lift the next object. There was a pause. A downpour was coming, but work was yet to be done. Hands grasped weakly and without belief and carried goods uselessly around. Within the span of a minute, The Drunk appeared to have aged 40 years.

Lunch was called, and the frail legs towed a torn spirit with hand over mouth to a vacant room. There, at once, a torrent was released.

Men were just men; women were merely women, and time had simply caught up with a loveless life.

When all was done and done with, The Drunk lay still, breathing. A gentle inhale soothed, and a mild exhale comforted. Time slowed to normal with minutes to spare to gather the strength to stand again. Work beckoned, and to some, its voice was irresistible and gave life to weary, battered legs.

Miraculously, renewed energy moved throughout the body; any and all objects seemed even lighter than usual. The flow of all things had been more or less restored. There had been, however, a change of some kind. The heart had been wounded, and it had not had enough time to heal. The mind had forgotten, but the soul had not.

Soon, the warehouse's temperature appeared to drop ever so slightly. Its laborers seemed more and more foreign to The Drunk with each hour, their hearts continents away. They were harmless, but there was no certainty to that. Shoulders stood on guard against a gradually approaching threat. The body shuddered as time whittled away at its spirit beneath.

And work had made it more than bearable. It was tedious, but there were far more unpleasant things lurking in the moment. Weighty boxes needed hoisting; delicate merchandise required packaging, and a vast inventory called for organizing. It was all a return to breath, nature's healing salve.

As the long night drew on and on, working bodies slowed as stress sped up; faces contorted as spirits shriveled. Energy by any means was sought. Reasons were clutched to and chanted for inner power. If there were an opportunity to steal a soul, surely the chance would have not been passed up by a few at this point.

But time eventually gave way, and the end of the shift was called. With burning haste and high-strung nerves, The Drunk moved past the exhausted crowd, as to flee from a curse. To come so closely to the cluster of foreign bodies was to be next to sorrow itself.

Soon, an exit was made, and there was no time to wait for The Lover. Apologies would have to come later. A place to hideaway and stow one's self away from the world was all that mattered now. It was too early to return home where only bottles awaited, but in that moment, the mind recalled of a nearby walking trail. Hardly was it used, and it would be entirely abandoned during this time at the onset of dawn.

Within minutes, The Drunk had arrived, and the first steps towards a day of healing had been taken. A gentle path with modest hills guided the breath back to clarity of thought. The cool, crisp air had nothing to say or any judgments to make and would only blow on a head hot with worries and aches. The sun, too, never failed to greet anyone who would greet it. Many footsteps were taken.

And all wasn't so miserable. It wasn't pleasant either, to be sure. Past memories of true agony were the proof of the state of the present.

It was not bleak like the graying grass, but it was largely a void. And isolation was to wander in that void as a stranger.

Chapter Ten: A Stranger in a Void

Take some steps here; take some steps there. Find nothing. Yet every once in a while, one would hear a whisper while wandering and have no choice but to follow it. Questions would arise: What was that whisper? Why did it whisper? And why did it whisper to me? To chase answers was to have purpose again. To find the source of that whisper was to find life itself. The end may or may not reward in full, but it itself would eventually lead to a new whisper to keep one wandering forever and ever in the void, curiously.

A few hours elapsed. Thoughts drifted towards the weekend, and rest was sorely needed. A retreat into books and writing would restore lost energies and passions. There was, however, one problem: no meals would be present during this retreat without a walk to the local market as well.

The Drunk had regained composure after a few miles, and the trip was to be routine. Spirits were still dampened, but the simple act of handpicking vegetables carried a subtle, unspoken calmness with it. In the face of the surreal and absurd, the mundane was muted, yet in their absence, it was all-knowing and all-powerful.

Many more footsteps were taken; the market was now within sight. Nerves tightened. Eyes glued themselves to the ground. A basket was put in hand. A few pairs of feet shuffled by, and the fruit stand was visible and then within reach. The head poked out and upward. Two, four, five, eight people came into vision and at once became alien. Their threatening eyes buried themselves into The Drunk's forehead. Their hearts beat together as one cosmic being; its very soul was unwelcoming, and its mind was the source of fear itself.

Items were quickly snatched up with tremoring hands and thrown into the basket. The feet roached forward and around two corners to safety. Only an empty line of produce awaited, and a few vital breaths could be taken. The least possible was then grabbed with rising panic while a scurry was made down the row. At the end of the line, a mother and her two children were turning the corner and came into view. A young pinkish toddler was held in one hand with a basket in the other; a puffed-cheek boy towed from behind, both products of love.

Pure disgrace flushed through the heart. Hands pulled a thin, delicate hood over the head, during which a cheek was sharply turned. There had never been a single desire for children or shame for feeling so, but it was just then, in this exact moment, nature had made her selection painfully known to the unselected. One had been chosen for survival while the other had been written off as sterile and infertile.

A soul in distress continued across one final row to take the last of its needs before scuttering to the exit. A hand strangling ample bank notes forced it onto the counter, and stringy legs took off in retreat.

Down the street, a secluded bench was found where bags were promptly dropped and tears came to relieve. The pain was primal, and the mourning was dark.

At the end of it, a level of calm did return, yet a hollow was all that remained. It lay there motionless. There were no signs of breathing. A moment passed.

In an instant, a sudden cackling broke out. It convulsed in short bursts of amusement and pleasure without reason or rhyme and at no apparent joke at all. The fit was uncontrollable and grew ghastlier with each snicker produced. A face worn and sagging with grief seconds ago was now grinning ear to ear in manic ecstasy. Tears of joy came forth and held just as much authenticity as the ones from sorrow. Then, a mix of coughing and laughter was released forcibly in order to make way for the deepest of breaths. And the relief was ever so sweet.

Chapter Ten: A Stranger in a Void

Euphoria had faded just as quickly as the heartache preceding it, and in a blink and a flash, it was as if nothing had taken place at all as though a gap in time had been cut and erased permanently. All was at peace again. The moment had recovered its beauty. Meanwhile, the legs had regained their strength; bags were to be carried, and a walk was yet in store. There was no further need to wait, so once more, The Drunk stood and began to make way.

The sun was now beating down fiercely on an already scorched road. Each ray and beam seemed to give life to hips swaying in the heat. There had been hotter days, and this one was no longer particular in any way; it was simply a day.

The mind was utterly clear and ready for a drink to wind down and prepare for bed. The idea of a dram had whispered its way in with its suggestive tone carrying a hint of seduction to it. Naughty lips arose, playful like children. The day never felt quite complete without a couple of glasses, and there was still time and more to enjoy.

The Drunk arrived home at last and swiftly started arranging for a hearty meal. Vegetables were cut and frying while sauces were stirred and stewing.

To wait was all that was needed; a drink would, then, pass the time. With glass in hand, stairs were climbed to the office. The smell of a strong Speyside scotch started to fill the room. To wait anymore now seemed pointless. The first sip was downed, and a large sigh came up along with thoughts of delicious malt and toasted barley; it was sweet and oaky. Yet it all faded within mere seconds. It was utterly gone and had taken all feeling with it, leaving only its absence to be felt. To sit with it was immediately disturbing. Another sip or two was taken, bringing back the flush of emotions from before. Savory spices coated the mouth fully where it sizzled and overpowered the mind with pleasure. The swallow redoubled all sensations down the throat until it ended with a loving embrace at the pit of the stomach. Soon again, feelings passed, and their impermanence brought gut-wrenching grief. Waiting for more was meaningless when more could be had sooner. The last of the glass was bottomed out and refilled straight away with a highly potent cask-strength bourbon. Eyes fixated on droplets clinging to the sides, flowing down to the pool of whiskey below. Anticipation spiked. The drink was thrown back with conviction, giving way to heavy corn, vanilla sweetness, and barrel bitterness, all enriched by the extreme proof in alcohol. The mind buzzed with a glee it could find nowhere else. Paralyzing joy rang through the body and wholly consumed the spirit. The effect rippled and rippled, and the heart pulsed and pulsed with love. Eventually, its warm presence began to disappear once again, and a creeping shadow cast itself upon the room. Without hesitation, a bottle of corn whiskey was snatched, planted onto the work desk, and popped with momentum. Lips met feverishly and inhaled a gulping or two. Satisfaction tingled across the face while a perfect numbing took hold all elsewhere, sending The Drunk into the unknown. Time ceased as another bottle stood unabashedly on a stack of papers, and it, too, was delicious. The head swirled in stupor and bobbled aimlessly while trying to decipher whether it was ready for more. And more was indeed desired. A swig was followed by a second swig, which was followed by a third swig. There and then, it was complete; the mind, body, and spirit united in total blankness, unable to even sit any further. The chair fell over, and The Drunk's cheek gently met with the desk itself where the arms instinctively reached out to embrace. Hands stroked the legs softly, feeling up and down with increasing warmth and shallow, rapid breathing. The whole of the desk was clung to, and the body brought itself closer to its rock. It was both nurturing and protective, seductive and charming, and tender and indomitable. The world was collapsing into darkness, and all that was holy stood

Chapter Ten: A Stranger in a Void

fast and strong with delicate arms stretched out ready to catch those in need. Fear that a grave mistake had just taken place produced a helpless calling towards the mother and the father, childishly begging for forgiveness. A terrible sin had been committed, and thus, judgment would be passed. The Drunk clutched and released and clutched again in waves of intensity, for the end was nigh. The maiden listened and soothed and hummed a tune of heart and soul, and her robust, sturdy body gave courage in the last moments. And all quickly blurred into a pit of a sunless void.

CHAPTER ELEVEN:

DEMON

Eyes awoke but remained shut. The body lay frozen in bed, fully intent on delaying the inevitable for as long as possible.

Pots and pans left simmering by The Drunk had been charred into complete ruin and later safely discarded by The Gambler before further damage could take place. Knowing this, the day ahead was ripe for wasting.

Sleep alternated with wakeful numbness, a state where no feeling could reside and thoughts did not exist.

In the place of the usual morning of undisturbed bliss at the desk, there was instead a vacuum of space to float through. The prone body sank then softly rolled and glided gently at an angle towards the heavens. It was far out of reach; yet it was an ideal always worth pursuing, for it was not a destination but a path heading nowhere yet always somewhere forward and never back. There were neither clocks in this space nor the anxieties they brought.

There was, however, a growing sense that this place was fleeting and would soon perish. The feet kicked outward from the

Chapter Eleven: Demon

bed and propelled the body to nowhere faster out of spite. There was nothing to run from, only a dream to run with. It was surreal to swim through a reality just as real as any other where nothing was anything and nobody was anybody. Here, society was a lie, and spirits were without a face and body to lord over others with. Movement, even if imagined, was truth in this space; it liberated the mind from itself.

Soon, bodily energy began to return and its restlessness along with it, yet the mind was free and didn't want to ensnare itself in the world once more. Fantasy carried no burdens and could fulfill any desire unfulfilled elsewhere. Thus, the body shifted, turned, and levitated at an angle downward to grasp at something new and quite different from before. It was alluring, warm, passionate, and shameless with an ability to pierce words and even subvert their meanings. Its elusiveness and unconscious nature made it completely inaccessible in waking life but utterly seductive in this space. Coming in and out with waves of full bodily pleasure, the sensations sometimes caused tremors and spasms when true connection could be imagined. And it was all imagined with arms tightly tucked around a pillow, fighting to prolong a dream.

But it was time. The vacuum of space had dissolved into full consciousness, and life was to continue. Hips gradually rocked the body until it was upright where the hands braced themselves against the bed for support. A few shallow breaths were taken, and then, The Drunk arose and stood once again.

A mirror was sought after out of sheer curiosity. It was at that moment when horror revealed the consequences of the prior day. The entirety of the neck was coated in a solid crimson red. Shock spread across the body and sent the mind into terror. Right away, the face was examined in a frenzy and appeared to have aged 10 years overnight. The chest seemed relatively normal and unharmed, but panic continued to escalate when the eyes returned to the neck and its fully flushed sanguine appearance. It had the look as if it had been violently strangled during the night, and it smelled of death. Damage had been made visible for all to see, the degree of which remained largely unknown. Questions drowned the mind in misery, giving way to an imagination to turn towards insanity. From the chaos, only one conclusion could be clearly made: if it were all to happen again, it would happen all the more so, and The Drunk would surely die.

Coming out into the common area, The Gambler was spotted standing with his back turned, closing the door to his private quarters.

"Gambler! Please, I have to ask you a favor. Do you have space available in your room?"

The Gambler gazed upon a broken face full of desperation. "I might, yes. What's wrong? You don't look well at all."

"I did a terrible thing. I drank and drank, and I couldn't stop myself. Something took over me, and I wasn't the one in control anymore. Do you see my neck? Look at it. Look at it closer. If it happens again—I won't. I can't. If you don't take all of my liquor, I will gladly pour all of it down the drain, all of it, one bottle after another."

"No, I'll take them. There's no need to do that with that kind of collection. I'll turn it into a great display one day."

"Are you sure? Your room is large, but it already holds so much."

"It will hold as much as I need and want. So, come, let's do it now."

Two boxes of bottles shifted from one room to the next, followed by two more boxes, which was then followed again by two more and two more to finish.

"Relief. God, what a relief. It's gone. I can breathe again. I'm finally free from it."

Chapter Eleven: Demon

"That must be over 100 bottles I counted. You must have been carrying that weight for years, I imagine. So then, I wonder, when did it all start? How long did it take to get to this point?"

"That's—hard to explain. It's been five years, but then, why, right? Why did I need so many? Why did I have to own them all? And when you have two or three bottles stashed around somewhere all the time, it's proof, you know? With that, you can say, 'I am not an alcoholic,' and you yourself believe it. Your inner world might be a sinking ship, but you have something else to find the meaning in everything burning down around you, a dream, a hope, a voice of love; but it's all so distant and unbearable to hold out and wait for, so unbelievably unbearable. So you buy more. You want more. And I couldn't stop seeing her—she won't leave me alone."

"Who's she?"

"Me. She is me. She's the one I murdered all those years ago, and we were only 16. I never thought she would ever come back, and then, one day, she did. And she did not want us to be whole. No. She was full of hatred for me and wanted the absolute worst for us. When I strangled her—back then, I made a promise to string myself up, too, but that promise had the opposite effect. It calmed me down just enough so that I could distract myself, knowing there was an exit, and it never quite happened. She, though, she remembered, and when she woke up after all those years of a false life, all I could see was us hanging and drooping in every room I went; those eyes always staring at the floor. Oh, she haunted me. Yes, she did. The very moment she came back to life the false person melted straight off my face, and she traveled from my mind down my neck and down my chest and finally landed in the pit of my stomach, causing everything to swell and quake with her memory, my memory. After the first minute of standing in shock, I lost the strength to stand any longer and could only lie in bed, awake for days, waiting to die.

"But of course, that didn't happen either. The months that followed saw more bottles and more of her. For a week, I swear, if I had looked in the mirror, my heart would have given out from fear alone. My face and body had become a man's and had lied to my soul for 20 years.

"Then, unbearable pain and time wore me down to a place I've only been once where love has never been and its absence is all that can be felt. Like a dying dog, I found the darkest room underground I could and sat on its floor. I was ready then. She gained complete control over my hand as I watched it seek by itself. Anything sharp would do, but there was nothing for it to grab. My legs were still mine but paralyzed, and so we sat together and bonded as one in terror and agony. An hour later, the thought of water came to mind, and with a single sip, all had returned to normal with only the memory of what had just happened.

"Eventually, years later with treatment, we did become whole, yet right, the whiskey never left. We are stitched together by the soul, but she has decayed and only moves from time to time. And oddly, I am happy. But she wants to love and be loved; and that is the most difficult thing in the world."

There was silence. While The Drunk had spoken, The Gambler had turned his head slightly away and fixated his eyes on a singular point on a wall far away, only allowing for a quick pivot at the neck here and there to refresh. During the silence, his eyes continued to stare at the wall as a mind calculated a response. No answer seemed to come at all. More silence passed. Suddenly then, there was a thought.

"Well, I do thank you for the new liquor cabinet."

The Drunk broke into a soulful chuckling while The Gambler smirked in satisfaction.

Chapter Eleven: Demon

"Yes, please, by all means. I don't think I'll need it anytime soon: the road to recovery will be quite long. For years, I've holed up in some wall from place to place and buried myself with endless work and never needed anymore than that, besides a drink. Money was needed miserably, and it was the only order in my life, which had completely collapsed upon itself. Treatment is very costly, and I don't even have enough now. But I do have a chance, and I have to take it. So the point is I must go. Regret and temptation is all I see here."

"Where will you go?"

"Faraway to a place where there are others, not similar but exactly like me. There, we share the same struggle. There, community is possible. If there is a place I belong and am better able to make peace with myself, it would be nowhere else. We see each other, and no one is without a face anymore. Even love is possible."

"You should go, then, yes. As much as I enjoy our feasts together where you rattle off the story behind everything you drink, I sit there and think to myself, 'I'm watching someone slowly but surely die by poisoning themselves willingly.' But I know your situation. Get whatever treatment you need. People who tell you not to don't have to deal with the consequences, which you already have. But before you go, allow me one story of my own.

"Years and years ago, I had been given a ticket to leave the country and to far off elsewhere to live, work, and study for an extended amount of time. I chose Berlin. And I could truly not have asked for more because it was bought and paid for by my family. All of it went to waste, however; nothing came from what was handed to me. I had dropped my schooling first year, spent every coin I had on gadgets and gizmos to distract myself with and did nothing but talk and drink with friends there.

"Managing to squander so much left me with wanting nothing but to throw myself into a deeper isolation. I then moved to Switzerland, telling my friends and family my intention to learn Swiss German; and there was some honesty to this as I had begun my studies again, but there was also a larger truth lurking in the darkest part of my mind. Times have changed, and while you may now be open with your desire, there are some that have gone into hiding long ago. So—I wanted to be utterly alone and reach a new low point, and just maybe, then, that would be enough to have the courage to throw it all away and be done with it.

"Months passed by. I remember sleeping the most I ever had before. It was the only state I could stand living in. I slept 16 on average but would take all 24 if it were possible, and it was some days. To be awake was to be in pain. Suffering and courage share the same bed and mate together; their children then have their own children and beget and beget until the day you are ready. When that day comes, something truly extraordinary happens. For the first time in a long time, you'll have a miserable form of spiteful energy to begin to plan and gather everything you need. You plot how and where it is to be done over the course of many days because it's all still so exhausting to tell you the truth.

"It was then one night shortly after a joyless meal that I became violently ill. What began with stomach pains gave way into terrible shakes and soon loss of all my bodily strength. Bed-ridden, then, with only a wall to keep me company, my body turned out everything it was holding. After the ninth or tenth trip to relieve myself, I couldn't move any longer and had no choice but to lie there instead. Everything burned and kept burning and burning inside of me. Moaning and crying do very, very little, but what else can you do while in the middle of a raging inferno? Then, extreme agony while curled up in a puddle of my own blood and filth left me to finally betray everything I believe in. I talked to God and

Chapter Eleven: Demon

begged him for death. I begged and I begged. This was exactly the moment I had been waiting for, and I was so close to what I wanted.

"Some time, perhaps an hour, passed by, and to say nothing happened would be an utter lie. Time spent alive only increased the pain, which made the wait far beyond unendurable. I had no more will to wait and suffer for that which I wanted more than anything, and so a new thought came directly to my mind, a single thought that changed the entire course of my life: I finally wanted something more than I wanted to die, which had been my greatest desire for years; my only wish, then, was for the pain to stop.

"A newfound life took over me, and from there, the idea and strength to crawl towards the door, to open it, and to beg for help slowly started to build over the course of the next hour. Life had never been uglier, but it was done.

"I'll never forget the day when I could walk again. I wandered the town in the dead of night, feeling as a ghost, passing by lifeless buildings, taking in their blueness from their moonlit presence, and asking why incessantly. Why? Why was I allowed to live? Why was I made to live? Was it God who ordered me to live? Of course not. Let's not get carried away; remember who you are talking to. But I will tell you. There was a reason, or there had to be a reason for me to want to live again. And maybe that is just a feeling, and even if so, I full-heartedly believe in that more than anything else in this greedy, self-serving world.

"So ever since, I've vowed to use this mind given to me and to make something of it, to make the best from it. I may take back what's mine and more from the casino; I may easily squander all my money even, but at least it will be my own money and no one else's and certainly not my life either."

A long pause ensued. The Drunk stood dumbfounded without a word in mind. The Gambler's unyielding spirit had filled the room entirely, leaving space for nothing else.

Two worlds had gathered as two sad and lonely roads converging and vanishing into an overgrown meadow of birds, bliss, and bees. All was connected again, and it was warm. Deep breaths were taken. The long pause had now begun to overstay its welcome.

"You gambled your life away only to win it back and more."

"I suppose so, yes. My family said something about me had changed when I came home, but they could never put their finger on it, especially when they don't know. Anyway, ought you to be going soon? Of course, you are free to come back whenever you are ready to. Visit me sometime, you hear?"

"I will, then. There is just one last stop I need to make before I go."

CHAPTER TWELVE:

THE LOVER

The Drunk approached the table, the usual meeting place, and there, it was The Lover who stood awaiting.

"I'm sorry I disappeared the other day."

"It's OK. I got your message, and I know your plans. You are going through quite a lot, aren't you? I want to say that you were doing so well getting back into the world, and then—I saw it on your face the other day right before you left. There was this withdrawing look you gave when you went into your own head, and it changed your entire energy—and not for the better. You retreated into your world of self-oppression. I know it when I see it because I used to do the very same."

"Do you expect me to not have thoughts? Feelings?"

"You could have fought it, don't you see? But you allowed yourself to dwell on it."

"If I didn't, that kind of thought would come back hours later or a day later or even years later. It would follow me like an ever so slowly moving but deadly shadow, and before I knew it, it would cut me down, like it has before. But I understand what you really mean to say, however. I know what you're going to say before you've even gotten the chance. I know that voice from you by now. You really wish to say that those feelings of disconnection will follow me wherever I go, no matter what treatment I receive."

"Your problem is internal."

"It's external as well. Without any treatment, my liver would have given out a long time ago. If I cannot embody my heart and soul, what is the point of living? If I cannot even connect with myself, how can I expect to connect with others?"

"Those disconnected feelings will never leave you. They are you, in fact. You must do the work yourself to fix the internal. In the end, that is what you will see."

The Drunk was visibly taken back. "Those feelings may never leave; you're right. But to the end, I'll go anyway. I may even chase beauty, but don't we all in some form or another, especially you? You chase it wherever it may drag you, and what's wrong with that? Why not keep chasing it as long as there is a stupid smile on your face and a head full of hope? What could be more beautiful than that? At that point, why would you listen to anyone telling you otherwise?"

There was an awkward pause while the two were at a standstill. The Drunk then continued.

"I may never be completely content with myself, and I am OK with that; but you know, I have felt it before, true connection, I mean. It is so rare in my life, and it never lasts for very long. It's been so many years since I've foolishly fallen for a girl, knowing I could never make her happy in the end. But I want to believe again. I want to believe that love is more than just a transaction. I want to believe there is someone who could be more than just flesh. No, I do believe it. Your stories are always such a treat, you know? You encounter this girl and then that one, and your eyes are so full of fiery ambition. Before I go, would you happen to have one more romance to share?"

Chapter Twelve: The Lover

The Lover hesitated. He slowly took in a deep breath as to find the proper moment. An instant ticked by. He began.

"I have realized now more than ever something that I've known but haven't seen all along: that I am now in the middle of a desert. And it is so dry and brutal here. Women—love attention, crave it, in fact, but want nothing more from me. I give them that attention with gifts and letters and poems, and they'll happily take it all. Yet as soon as I ask for their hand in return, there is only coldness to be found, the coldest of feelings, which houses their truest opinion of me. It's all so heartless, and I can't bear it anymore. No, I don't want your sympathy, and I don't need it either. I'm not that pathetic. But I'll tell you what is pathetic: a man in similar circumstances would seek wealth and power and status, almost as a means of revenge, and they would have all the intensity necessary to succeed, too. A man who is hungry, truly hungry, becomes a mad beast. And from the urban wilds, he will emerge with as much as he needs and advertise it to all who would care, and he himself will become the lover of attention and come to crave it. And worst of all, it will in turn attract women that do not love him for what he has and especially not for who he is. A heart-broken woman will take security over romance as long as the price is right. Give it a year, maybe two, a marriage and children, and then watch it all collapse like twigs crackling and roasting into ash in an open fire. How moronic, how fat-headed do you have to be to think otherwise? That is utter desperation. That is not a man who loves women but a man who loves satisfying only himself. His children will grow to hate him; his wife will take everything she can, and his bitter ego is all that will remain. Now, that is pathetic.

"No, I am not that hopeless. Here, then, is the story you asked for. This one, too—lingers. Many months ago, I received a message from a girl I knew from my group of peers who had moved away to a different city for her education. She was breathtakingly beautiful, one of the most pristine faces I've ever seen in person. Truly, she was doll-like all around. I was terrified to say even one word to her. But I had gotten to know her over the several months she was kind enough to attend our gatherings at cafes and bars. There, her outlook and attitude stood out just as much as her presence did. Many from our group often complain or bicker or even just endlessly recount their day to day lives as matters so important that the whole of us ought to know as if no one had any matters quite as urgent.

"And politics was always a bad idea. Something about it brings out the worst frustrations people have with themselves so that they can channel it away into some external target to throw hate upon. And any deviation that was not part of the groupthink was a bad start to something that did not end well. Then, there were these talks of how people should and should not be that had me clenching my fists, wanting to shout the truth of the dark, unchanging reality of humanity. These people—these—professional grumblers and bellyachers were not after truth or beauty and instead could only say all things unattractive.

"This girl I speak of, however, participated in *none* of this. She was far too wise to even raise a hand to any of this tomfoolery. No, whenever her mouth opened, it was to do good. Her tenderness and warmth were her virtues. And there was no falseness to her positivity; it was *genuinely* her. And I'll tell you something you've known all along: there is nothing more attractive in this world than authenticity.

"Where there are hundreds and thousands of people we encounter who are trapped in the throes of their lives, she seemed calm and collected through it all. But she was not immune herself. No one is, after all.

"A few months after our first meeting, I got talking to her one day in private while away from the group; she only then revealed

Chapter Twelve: The Lover

her story and a life of blistering turmoil. All had culminated into a single night where she had made her way to the rooftop of a hospital and was perched on the edge along with several empty bottles of wine. She put her life into the hands of fate, and fate merely put her to sleep safely that night.

"It was then shortly after our talk that she moved away, but not two days after, I received that very message I spoke of earlier. In it —she confessed that she had an interest in me. And I couldn't believe it. I *didn't*, in fact. I refused to even. I wrote her back, complimenting her on her sense of humor and then carrying on our conversation as normal. She immediately wrote back to double down her interest in me and was very overt with her desires. And that undid something inside of me that I never even knew existed at all until that moment. My entire body ached all over for her, and it quaked; and it quaked. For the first time ever in my life, I was vulnerable. She was the one who could hurt me. Her invisible hand hovered over my heart to caress it with the power to crush it at any time. The pit of my stomach caved in and trembled with pure desire for all of her and nothing else. I couldn't eat. I couldn't sleep. I was rendered useless at work and could only have waking dreams of her. For days, this continued until the crash finally washed over me, leaving me chillingly cold and numb without her.

"I wrote her back during my unraveling, and I asked her why over and over. Why did she like me? She was so painfully beautiful that she could easily have had anyone she wanted in our group, even the world. I asked her what she wanted from me, a short, ugly, lonely pile of nothing. Was it money, or was it information? Because it was not me she wanted. And I told her outright, 'I *will* ask you my 1,000 questions because I have to because you are dangerous to me.'

"Her reply was only that she wished for me to talk with her— nothing more. So I did. We then talked about our past pains and uncertain futures and hungers in life, and it was all mixed in with a sultry mood. Just writing to her and reading her messages filled me with the same bloody warmth from before, only it was now more than manageable.

"Later, I offered to take the next train ticket to go see her, but she was buried beneath a brimming and burdened schedule planned for several weeks ahead. My only option was to keep talking with her, and so I did. Eventually, however, I could sense it, and the thought couldn't escape me: her interest was fading away little by little. She was responding less and less, not necessarily with her words but her emotions. Perhaps, she grew bored of me or had met someone else; or perhaps, it was pity for me all along, and it had come to an end. I'm not sure I'll ever know.

"But let me tell you something: whether or not her intentions and character were truly that pure, cherry, and sinless, I had imagined them to be. I had fallen for something I had completely thought up, and I would happily fall for it all over again. I live to long for that day. It was the truest thing I've ever experienced, and all else now seems as a lie in comparison."

The Lover nodded gently several times with total conviction, and there was silence. The Drunk blushed with soft feelings across the cheeks. The table radiated the baked glow it had absorbed from the mellow sun. Time passed.

"You know, the church offers a program as a means of therapy for drunks like me, but I find more therapy in stories like ours more than anything else. Maybe I'll go one day just for the stories."

"Do you believe in God?"

The Drunk hesitated. "If I say yes, people will take that to mean I'm religious, but I'm not. The more I seek religion or religion seeks me the more I find the truth about people rather than about god. But now, after everything, the idea that there is something much larger and greater than you is holy. To surrender

Chapter Twelve: The Lover

to something, anything, that has always been and always will be is beautiful. It's peaceful. I believe in the idea of god, yes, but I'll have to write my own scripture instead. So I will. And it will be a paradox, like me."

ABOUT THE AUTHOR

Ember White has traveled the world, looking for the place where she belongs, but it was not until she started reading that she was able to find her true home inside books.

She is now an author and publisher who writes under many names. Her previous work "The Boy Who Wanted to Be a Deer" is now available.

Printed in Great Britain
by Amazon